The Butterfly

Mind,

Edited by P Goulding

Chapters

I was surprised that I could dream about her like it was any other night. After everything that had happened. It was like my subconscious didn't care. Did that mean I didn't care? Well, no, of course I did. And yet, I dreamt like I always did. It was waking up that was the problem. Facing the next day. Facing my family. Facing the doctors and therapists. Facing the other patients on the ward.

Telling one of the younger female staff members: "I don't belong here, I think I should be able to go home" was probably the worst thing I could have done. She just smiled and said she would talk to one of the doctors. I didn't realise that saying that would actually make me look even less stable and lead to me being kept there longer. How come they were the ones with the power to tell me when I could leave? It didn't make any sense. But then again, none of it did.

At least I had stuff to keep my mind occupied. Stuff to stop me from reliving it all over again... That night. It was only two nights ago, and although it was still so fresh, I could tell that it was a night that I would never forget. I would look back on this day as the day that changed everything. Because everything had needed changing.

I had gone to eat breakfast and was sitting in the small dining area when one of the younger male doctors came in to check everyone's mood. The middle aged woman who had checked on me before hadn't said anything. She had just watched me and taken notes. This guy was new – or at least he seemed it to me – and was making sure not to miss any details. He saw me and looked on the list again, as if to say "who are you then?"

I guess the other doctors hadn't told him yet. Shit.

"Erm, hi, can I take a name?" he said, oddly shy. He was actually very handsome. Short, blonde hair and a well-defined chin. Muscly, but still slim. I looked down to the floor to avoid his eye-line but glanced up quickly. I wonder if he could tell that I was attracted to him.

"A... ask the other doctors... please", I managed to say. I felt like an idiot. What even was that?

"Oh, ok. Sure." He looked confused, but he clearly knew by now not to question strange behaviour in a place like this. The rain outside seemed to pick up the pace and the noise was loud around us. I was starting to feel so awkward. I just wanted him to move on to the next room of patients. Leave me alone. Leave me alone. I didn't know what to say.

"E... everyone calls me Beam." The words fell out. "As in a beam of sunshine... You can call me that if you want." Oh my god, I was flirting. I couldn't believe it... In a place like this. After everything that had happened.

"Ok, Beam. Nice to meet you. I'm Dr Martin," he said with a genuine smile, before walking out the door. Of course, that name wasn't on the list he had in front of him, but I felt rude not introducing myself at all.

I looked back down at my breakfast. It was actually really nice. I had been dreading the thought of hospital food so much, but I was pleasantly surprised. I had bacon, eggs, beans and chips. Today was only a Thursday and yet we were being served a fry-up! A strange pang of guilt hit me, as I thought of tax payer's money being spent on my breakfast. Did I even deserve this? No, I didn't. Not after what I had done. The guilt worsened and gradually I completely lost my appetite. I pushed the plate away, but then I noticed one of the cooks watching me and she began pointing and whispering something to one of the other staff members. Oh right, I had to eat. They would check my plate. They would ask questions.

I picked up the fork and tried to force the bacon into my mouth. Then a girl around my age walked in. She was holding a guitar and looked extremely absent, as if she was surrounded by a thousand fairies that

4

made her dizzy. I tried to catch her eye, in an effort to make friends, but she was miles away. I wondered why she was here. She didn't look insane or too thin. Or anything. Just normal.

Then I realised I would look fairly "normal" to her if she even saw me. Maybe I looked a bit worn out. But just like any other patient in here. True. I wanted to talk to her. I hated feeling so lonely in here. I just couldn't catch her eye. After trying a couple more times, I thought I would give up. It's not like she was going anywhere. I could talk to her another time.

"No! Fuck no!" boomed a voice from outside. It was loud enough to get this other girl's attention too. Yet, still with a gazed look on her face, she looked through the open doorway that was directly behind her. The brunette ponytail cascading from her head gently flicked as it fell from behind her shoulders.

"Calm down. Just calm down Samantha" a doctor said in a soothing voice, but it only seemed to freak her out further. Two other doctors ran in and grabbed an arm each. One of them was the hot doctor from before. It was the first time I had seen something like this – although I had been expecting it. There were about twenty patients in the ward in total, some with more severe mental conditions than others. I constantly tried to reassure myself that I was of course one of the less mentally ill patients, but what worried me was that everyone in here seemed to do the same. Samantha was taken to her room and everyone on the ward continued like nothing had happened. I heard her lock her door as loud as she could. All the patients' rooms locked from the inside, but the staff had a key anyway. The locks were really just to make us feel safer – that's all.

I had to get out. Even if it meant pretending that I was a completely normal person. Just as that fleeting thought ran through my head, a therapist came out from the therapy room. It was built deliberately in the centre of the ward. The main sitting area was next to it, where most of the patients sat and stared at the TV all day. I couldn't say for certain that they were watching it, just staring at it. One patient enjoyed singing along to the music channels so loudly that the ward staff had to send him to his room. The singing, however, would not stop. I was scared that the other patients would kick off or something, but instead, some smiled, others joined in. One stood up silently and left to go to his room. But no one seemed disturbed or surprised at this elderly man's attempt at singing Little Mix. In fact, he was rather talented for an old man.

"Next it's..." The therapist's sentence trailed off. She turned to face me. "It's your turn darling", she said gently. I smiled. How kind. She must have really liked me. I felt the safest I had for a long time in that small moment.

"Ok, do I need anything?" I was used to saying that for job interviews, or meetings at school. Always ask if you're expected to bring something. A notepad. A pen. But here, in this context, the question seemed almost sarcastic. I had nothing. Barely any possessions at all. The therapist just walked back into her office, expecting me to follow her. So I did.

I walked into a small room with too many people in it. They were all sitting around in chairs like the patients on the ward, but they were clearly different. They were doctors, therapists and other staff that I hadn't seen on the ward yet. They didn't stare, they watched. They didn't sing, they whispered. They didn't smile, only nodded. I sat. They were analysing me. Every movement. Each one of them gave off an aura of superiority.

The main therapist, who I assume was in charge of the rest of the staff, was a small, thin lady. Many of her colleagues were double her size. She wore a black blazer with sleeves that were rolled up so far that they only came down to her elbows. Her hair was in a tight bun with a small black band around it. Her shoes were stylish, but simple. She looked like a PA to a CEO rather than a doctor. Then again, what does a doctor in a mental ward look like anyway?

"So, how are you feeling?" asked the main therapist. It was uttered in the most condescending and pitiful tone that I had ever heard, and yet, it was still somehow comforting. It made me want to explain everything. But that was not going to happen. No way. Not here. Not now. I couldn't. No way.

"To be honest, it's all very overwhelming being here. But, if it's going to help me get my life sorted, then I don't mind. Obviously, that's all I want." I tilted my head gently to the right and faked a small smile. I felt like I was performing for them. GCSE Drama paid off. They were waiting for me to fuck up. But I wouldn't. I would keep it together.

"And how is it you would like us to help you achieve that?"

"Well, therapy to help me deal with the issues I have in my head would help, I think. If that's what you think? To be honest, I'm not sure I want to start taking anti-depressants. Not if I can get better myself." I could feel the words start to tumble out, so I stopped there.

"Therapy won't be a problem, of course not. That's what we're here for. You seem like a very positive, happy… person. How did you get yourself into all this, eh?" piped up one of the other therapists. She was larger and wore scruffy clothes. Her hair fell recklessly down, covering her face. Was she allowed to talk to me in such a condescending way? No one challenged her, so I guessed she was.

"It just all got too much. The realisation of what I am. Obviously, deep down I have always known that one day I would have to deal with the shit… oh sorry, deal with the stuff going on in my head. But it got to a point where I couldn't run away anymore. And knowing that I had to deal with everything just seemed so… so…"

"Scary?" another therapist suggested. Her hair was cut short, and she was slightly chubby. She was the first therapist that actually looked me in the eyes. She seemed genuinely gentle and understanding. I felt like I could trust her. To tell her everything in the hope that she could make it all better. I wanted a friend.

I looked down. I wanted the questions to stop but they had only just begun. The main therapist stopped writing notes and put down her pen. Then she looked up.

"Ok, well, this all seems standard enough for now. We will have to put you on anti-depressants and keep you here for another couple of days. You will be able to leave when we are convinced you won't try anything stupid again. Can you promise us that you won't? Ok? You are so young. You promise? We'll do one hour of therapy a day, and we will arrange for you to see the psychoanalysis expert. You can go off site with a member of staff, but not on your own yet. Does that all sound fair?" She wasn't asking me. She was asking the room. Her large group of subordinates nodded. They were not going to argue with their boss. So it was set. I had no say at all, but I had never expected to, to be honest.

I continued to sit there while they continued to watch me closely, until I realised that I was meant to get up and leave. So I did. I couldn't tell if it had gone terribly, or perfectly. Later that day, I saw other patients go in and then come out crying that they were being held for another month. That really hit home. Maybe I wasn't crazy like this lot. Maybe I was just in a bad way. Regardless, if I kept this up, I would be home before I knew it. Work wouldn't need to know. Friends would understand. And my family... Oh fuck, my family. Every time I attempted to think about my family, a dark cloud of guilt surrounded my entire being, and I just couldn't face it. Not yet.

That evening, I was showering in my room when I heard a noise. My room was the only one with its own toilet and shower on the ward. I felt lucky, but then again, I could understand why I had it. Maybe the other patients were jealous, or maybe they didn't even notice. I didn't care. I was too busy enjoying my shower. The negative energy of the day was flowing off me and down the drain. It circled and tried to hold on to this world, but the force of the water dragged it away. It left me clean and a step closer to happiness.

Then I heard the noise again. It was coming from directly outside my room. I dried myself off with a towel, and looked through the small glass window in my door that the therapists used to check on us. They checked that we were sleeping at night by turning on a haunting red light every two hours or so. It made falling asleep difficult. Even when it woke me, I would pretend to be asleep so that they would think that I was ok. One of the other patients had told me to sleep facing the other side so that even if my eyes threw themselves open, only I would know.

After I was dry and in my PJs, I crept outside. Curfew wasn't for another couple of hours, and yet it seemed late in the day. The girl from earlier was outside, with her guitar. And now a boy was with her, around our age as well. They were playing the guitar and singing. It was outside in a kind of cage like extension for the smokers. I could smell it from my doorway, but luckily the smell of smoke had never particularly bothered me.

I didn't recognise the song that they were singing, otherwise I probably would have joined in. Instead, I just walked over to them smiling and waved gently. They turned to me and whilst smiling, they kept singing. It really was lovely. They seemed at peace and untouchable. The guy stopped playing the girl's guitar and rested it on the floor beside him. He was tall and thin, with jet black hair. He had a goofy look about him, but was still quite handsome. In a geeky kind of way. If you had seen him with the girl out in public it would have looked odd though. You would immediately know they weren't a couple. If they had been in the same secondary school, you could tell that she would be with the popular kids and he would be in the library. But in here they were friends. It was sweet.

"Hey, you alright?" he said. Charming. Very charming.

"I'm... good. Sorry, I couldn't help but hear the guitar. You guys seem really cool." I felt like I was in secondary school again.

"Aww, you are the cutest thing ever. Why are you in a place like this?" the girl asked. I felt like I could trust them, like I could tell them anything.

"I tried to kill myself a couple of nights ago."

"Oh shit, really? But you seem so happy?" He seemed shocked. I thought that attempting suicide would be seen as normal for patients here.

"Well, I guess, yeah. It's like I've been reborn I guess. I don't know, it sounds stupid. I had a lot of stuff going on in my head." I was starting to mutter so quietly, I even irritated myself.

"That sucks. I've been here for ages now. Therapist says it's not safe for me to be out there." He turned to face the other side of the smoker's cage. The main road leading to the hospital seemed to tease him with cars casually driving to and from it. The guy dropped his head and his jet black fringe covered the left side of his face until all I could see was the back of his neck. He didn't strike me as dangerous.

"What about you?" I said to the girl.

"Let's just say it's safer for me in here too." She deflected the question with an ease that had taken months to perfect. I could tell.

I stayed outside with them for what felt like hours. We talked and laughed, just like normal young adults did. Except that, every two hours, one of the staff on the ward would come and check on us. They took notes, and then carried on.

After a few days on the ward, it was finally time for me to leave. Georgina had come to pick me up in her small Ford, with flowers and a huge tub of ice cream.

"I bet you were dying in there with all that healthy food they must have had you on," she laughed. Georgina was my best friend, and had been for years. We had gone to the same secondary school together, and moved into a small flat together through college, along with two other roommates. We went on to get a smaller flat together when we both started working. It was a Saturday, so she could come and get me without taking time off. I'm sure she would have done it anyway, but I would have felt even guiltier.

"Thank you for coming Georgina." I sounded sad, but thankful.

"Don't be silly, you're my best mate, I will always be there for you. I just wish I had been before..." Her usual bubbly personality fell away. The guilt was too much for me to bear. I had to change the subject. Or maybe I should've faced it head on. It was still all so new to me. How was I supposed to react to people?

"I... I hope you brought spoons!" I joked. Awkwardly. She just stared at me and forced a smile. She was always better at faking smiles than I was.

"Listen, I'm sorry. I'm sorry I couldn't see the signs earlier. You clearly weren't happy... even after everything we tried. I will do my best to be there for you from now on, ok?" Georgina said as she touched my arm. She looked me dead in the eyes and nodded. I could feel the cold droplets of water from the ice cream tub fall onto my already freezing finger tips, as the summer sun began to melt it. Soon it would be soup.

"Thanks. That's all I could possibly ask," I said with a smile. The engine started, and soon we were driving on the M25 back up to our flat in Camden.

It was the start of a brand new me – I had decided. I had to. I had no choice. It was time to face everything that I had run from for years. Everything would be fine, surely? I would put the past behind me as of this day. That would end up becoming the single most important day of my life.

The Main Stage was completely made of crystal and built over a river that stretched all the way to the Western end of the island. On a Summer's day, dolphins, merpeople and other wonderful creatures would swim up close to the stage – some even swam directly underneath it. They could be seen splashing under the crystalline light as the Queen took to the stage. But not today. Today was not a Summer's day. Instead, frozen blades of ice cascaded from the sky, one by one. They would fall with great power and speed, as they were larger than icicles in physical realms like Earth. In order to avoid any harm coming to the people of her nation, the Queen had cast a Veil of Warmth over her lands to reduce the icicles down to nothing but droplets of harmless water.

The Queen walked along, as the Main Stage drew closer and closer to her. Her people were clustered around it, standing and sitting all over the place, desperate to get a better view. She glided through them like a faery and they were all too awestruck to speak to her. She was, after all, the Queen. Queen Fubuki. Of course, even if they had tried to speak to her, or even approach her, they would have had to get past her Four Guardians. They had chosen for themselves the names of "Strength", "Endurance", "Agility" and "Defence". Each of these four deadly warriors stayed close to her whenever the Queen requested them to do so. Not that she needed them. The Queen was one of the most powerful, gracious and magickal beings in Macha Land. She could cast an array of different spells and her people loved her for it.

She closed in on the Main Stage and began to walk up the crystal steps as the crowd fell silent. Her Songshows were frequent, but they nevertheless captured the people's attention like nothing else. Great magic, wonderful music and merriment for all. The Queen truly knew how to put on a show. She would even try to ensure that the less fortunate of the nation were fed and watered with a conjuring spell. Whilst she could not provide for all, she did what she could. One evening she managed to conjure fourteen whole barrels of ale and the nearby villagers broke out into one of her songs in celebration.

The Queen ruled over what was known as Macha Land, and had done so for many, many years. She was a fair Queen who cared deeply for her people, and her knowledge of the arcane helped her to protect them. When her magickal energies were at their peak, she could summon fire and red lightning from nothing, or move tides and winds around her. She could also transform herself into the Phoenix. In this astral world, things were not bound by the laws of physics. Instead, life itself was flexible and malleable. That was why the realm was hers to rule as she saw fit.

She had sleek black hair, with two shorter cuts for her fringe that hugged her oval shaped face. Half of her hair was done up in a bun and the rest cascaded effortlessly down. The bun was held together by two silver needles, decorated with chains and bells that sang in the night.

Her people's favourite outfit was her pure white robe. At her neck, it cut into what looked like the lapels of a suit jacket, but folded into itself like a Yukata. The sleeves were long and flowed down from her hands to her knees. The dress continued down in a simple white fountain of fabric. It was held together with a thick red ribbon, which matched the rubies that she wore. The ribbon was simple at the front of the dress, but behind was folded into a wonderful bow. Depending on her mood and the occasion, the Queen would carry either her golden staff, or her three swords. Today she chose her swords – two large ones and one small. The two larger swords were a metre and a half long, one black and one white, with metal so sharp it could fly through stone, like a breeze cutting through the trees. The smaller dagger was the size of her forearm, curved and also exceedingly sharp. It was sheathed in a crimson, metal case. It lay by her right hip – rarely to be used. The Queen, of course, had no intention of using either these swords or her Four Guardians, but they helped encourage cheers from her nation.

As the Queen ascended to the stage, and walked elegantly to the centre of the gloriously wide crystal floor, she looked out over her realm. Macha Land was made up of three islands. The largest of which was where the Queen resided. It stretched over the surface of the planet from North to South, and had formed as one large mass of land. The Queen could see, from atop the crystal stage, the Windy Planes to the West of the island, and the large river that ran through the capital. North of the capital was Queen Fubuki's Palace, made entirely of crystal, like the Main Stage.

She could see almost as far as the Southern Beaches. In the season of Summer, the Southern region of the island was known as the Southern Desert, because the heat caused the sands to reach for miles and miles. However, it was Winter, so the Southern Desert had reduced down to become the Southern Beaches, and only spread for a few miles. When Summer returned, so did the vast wastelands of sand. Each year saw the repetition of this natural phenomenon. Fubuki felt the cold winds coming from the grand Ice Mountain that stood to the East of the stage. In Summer it melted down to be nothing more than the Lake. The merpeople of Macha Land swam North to the Lake when it was warmer in Summer, and could be seen splashing about their charms and pearls by local fishing villagers. When the cruel, harsh winds of Winter began to take over, the entire clan would swim South to the Southern Beaches, to enjoy whatever heat remained in the realm.

The other two islands were so small and lifeless that the Queen declared herself ruler over those as well.

Naturally, she had no one to challenge her on this. The second largest island was South West and consisted merely of dust and sand. It was utterly uninhabitable. The last island was so small, that you would believe yourself capable of sailing around it in no more than a half-day. It was known as the Volcano Island and it was in the Western reaches of the planet.

When the crowd saw their Queen, they began to call out her name.

"Queen Fubuki!" one cheered. Then another. Suddenly, hundreds of her people were shouting her name.

"Queen Fubuki! Queen Fubuki! Our Queen!" The shouting continued.

She smiled, and threw her arms outwards as she began spinning on the stage. Her gown lifted from the ground and her sleeves flickered in the winds. The weighty swords flew off into the sky like shooting stars and exploded into a thousand sparks of light as they reached the Veil of Warmth. Her people gazed at the sky above her in awe. As Queen Fubuki began her Songshow, the waves beneath her started to stir, and small droplets of water floated upwards slowly towards the Queen. Her magickal energy was as strong as it could be. It was as if she had her own gravitational field. Blue spheres of water started to swirl around her as she slowly continued to spin on the spot. Her feet danced around each other and her hair blew effortlessly in the wind. The crowds went wild for her.

Her Guardians took their places. They spread out around the edge of the circular stage. Her gown had been transformed into a shorter, sexier outfit that allowed her to walk, run and dance. She would sing to her heart's content, and dance along with the wonderful music.

As the music continued, the Queen glided along the stage, singing to her people. She twisted and twirled, and her hair flowed softly behind her. The droplets of melted icicles rained down on her. She performed songs about freedom and love. Her voice was powerful and deep. Yet, it was soft enough to melt the hearts of the people. With every electric word, her fans were hypnotised. Magick carried her music across the vast fields that surrounded the Main Stage. In these fields, were the benches, tents and small camps from where her people watched the Songshow. Some came days beforehand to ensure a good place before the Main Stage.

Some of the richer villagers sailed there directly from the dock in the West, and anchored as close as they were able. The merpeople listened from the South. Forest faeries left the South Eastern woods in order to be there. While she sang, the rest of Macha land fell silent. The calm took over as every living creature listened to her peaceful voice.

She danced, and red sparks of lightning flashed underneath her feet. The white robe flowed behind her as she jumped in the air. She was at her happiest when she was dancing and singing. Her power was at its strongest. She felt untouchable. Invincible. Glorious.

Unfortunately, she was wrong. As she danced and sang, she saw people crowding around something at one of the furthest tents to the East. She could barely see what was happening, but she could instantly feel that something wasn't right. The music and the singing stopped as she lost her focus. She stared fearfully at the crowd in the distance. What was happening? Was someone... hurt?

"Queen Fubuki! Come!" She heard one of the villagers shout out. It didn't look like anyone was fighting. Whatever could it be? At once she hurried to the edge of the Main Stage. The crowd was still too far for her to jump down to. She had to fly there. The surrounding creatures of the realm watched on helplessly. An odd scream of fear could be heard in the background. Her heart sank. Where were her Four Guardians? Where was her Prince?

She didn't have time to look for them. In a heartbeat, she leapt from the Main Stage. The crowd gasped as she jumped into the air. Her hair fell out of its bun, and her white robe flapped behind her as she flew in the direction of the commotion. Just as it looked like she would plummet to the floor, the air around her filled with energy and she gently drifted down back onto her feet. She started to walk quickly to the scene. As she got closer, her nose was hit with a smell so terrible that she couldn't help but gag.

"My Queen! He is here. Please, help him!" An elderly woman sobbed at her. Her cries and tears muffled her words.

"What happened here?" Queen Fubuki asked. Her voice was calm.

"I don't know, my Queen. We were watching the Songshow, and then suddenly he was... he was... screaming. Violently. He couldn't take in air. And then the smell..." The woman became virtually incomprehensible. Queen Fubuki waved someone over to calm her down.

"Be still, my lady, I am here now." Queen Fubuki's nerves were starting to get the better of her.

She approached the dying man. He was shrouded by a mist of black. It was death. Death in a form she had not seen before. It was unnatural, forced and manipulated.

"Winds of healing, cast your light, cure this man on this cold night." Queen Fubuki's words were simple, but filled with a strong magickal energy. She was still empowered from the Songshow. She would not let an innocent villager die in front of her. And yet, her words resulted in nothing. The man continued to writhe and vomit.

"Be cured!" She tried again. White light glowed from her hands, and those around her looked away as it was too bright. "He will be cured!" She was almost screaming. As she did, a black puff of smoke in the shape of a man's face floated up from the man's body. It absorbed her light, and then burst into a violent spray of warm water. The water hit Queen Fubuki's skin, and she screamed in disgust. The man was dead. She could see his lifeless body on the floor.

The woman wailed behind her. It took three men to hold her back. Queen Fubuki was frozen still in fear. Never before had she failed to save one of her people. The realm of Macha Land had been at peace for as long as she could remember. All for nothing.

"Who did this?" Queen Fubuki bellowed into the air. "Who!?" She screamed with all her might. The voice echoed so loudly that the Ice Mountain in the distance bounced her words back at her. The echo filled the skies and carried on to the Southern Beaches. Queen Fubuki turned back to face her people. They all watched her silently. The vast area of tents and benches was still and quiet. She looked at the mourning woman.

"The Coven of Rosemary will take care of you and your kin. I will have them bring you anything you need that may ease your pain." She looked towards the corpse. "I will give this poor soul the end he deserves. A clean burial. Then, with all the powers I possess, I will avenge him. I will find whatever killed him and end its life in payment for his. I could not heal him and I cannot bring him back. Vengeance is all I can give to you."

With that, Queen Fubuki caught the eyes of her Prince in the distance. He was trying desperately to get to her, but he was too late. She walked over slowly to the already rotting corpse, and lifted it into her arms. The heat built within her. She was about to use her most powerful spell. She was about to become the Phoenix.

Orange and red flames spread from her feet and legs and within seconds she was aflame. Bright fiery strips of yellow and deep reds burned around her. They reached out to form her wings. She lowered her head and let the transformation take place. She let go of her human form, and turned into a magnificent bird. Her feet became claws, and her mouth a beak. She burned brightly. The fire was warming and radiant. In her claws, she kept the corpse held tight, and in a flap of flaming wings she launched herself into the air. Puffs of smoke followed behind her as she reached high up into the sky. The Main Stage was below her, as were her people. Prince Hikaru watched on, still in turmoil that he hadn't been able to reach her.

In a burst of crimson, the body exploded in the sky. She had cleansed it with fire, and destroyed whatever unnatural toxin had taken it. It burned away, and ash fell gently to the floor. As the beautiful red Phoenix floated in the air, she could see a strange figure in the distance, far in the East, by the Ice Mountain. She could see a shady black figure standing upon one of the flat cliffs on the side of the mountain. Was it a beast? Was it a shadow? Was it nothing at all? She did not know. What she did know, was that it filled her heart with an overwhelming feeling that this was not over. It had only just begun.

I had taken a week off work to do it. Georgina was down visiting her parents, so I had the place to myself. I had planned everything, so there was nothing to stop me. It was easy to lie to those around me because I didn't think I would have to deal with the repercussions. I was dead inside. I felt apathetic towards the world. In a weird way, I missed the lack of emotion I felt that night because it was easier to feel nothing, rather than feel all the pain and guilt I felt now. But now, I was different. I had made the choice to start afresh and carry on living as the new me. I was back at my flat in North London and next on my list, was to talk to Georgina. It was her that I worried about the most.

On Sunday night, I got everything ready for work the next day early, so that we could sit down and chat about things. We both felt like we owed each other an apology. Me, for putting her through something so awful, and her, for not noticing how bad things had been for me. She was a clever girl and my best friend. She knew I wasn't happy, but I don't think she ever imagined it was bad enough for me to try to kill myself.

"Beam, if I had known, do you not think I would have tried to stop you? Do you not think I would have tried to find a way to make you happier? You're my best friend, and the thought of losing you..." She began to tear up, so I put down my ice cream and reached for her hands.

"I know hun, it's ok. Don't get upset. I didn't want to hurt you anymore than I had to, that's why I tried to make sure you wouldn't be here. I wasn't myself, I haven't been for a long time now. But I want you to know, things will be different now. I am different now. I don't want to die anymore."

"I should fucking hope not!" Georgina shouted with her eyes wide open. It was hard trying to describe it to her, she had never felt that level of depression. I never wanted her to either. "It's all well and good waiting 'til I was away, but who do you think would have found you?"

"I know…" I looked down at the floor. She had a point. What could I say? I planned to be dead so I didn't care? No… I couldn't say that. It would hurt her too much. "I'm sorry, I didn't plan it very well." I lied. I had planned it extremely well. Too well even. If I hadn't panicked after waking up suddenly from my drunken slumber in the bath tub after taking those pills, it would have all ended very differently.

"Well, B, we can't change what happened. I feel just as bad that I didn't do anything to try and help you. So let's just try and take each day as it comes, and eventually aim to put this past us. Just promise me you won't do that again, ever." She squeezed my hands tight. Her pyjamas were covered in pink teddy bears, which made it hard to take her seriously. Her eyes met mine and she looked straight at me.

"Of course, I promise. Georgie, I'm different now, it's like I have my life back so I can finally do what needs to be done. A second chance. Ok?" I smiled sincerely.

"Good. Ok. Well, let's finish our ice cream, watch some TV and relax before work tomorrow. Do you need a lift to the station as usual?" Georgina put my ice cream back in my hand and unmuted the TV. We were watching a romantic comedy with our favourite male actor in it.

"That would be great, thank you hunny."

The next day I woke up before my alarm. The strange breakfast times on the ward had made me get up earlier than usual, and it clearly hadn't worn off yet. I lay there in bed thinking about what I would have to face today. I would have to tell my boss what would happen from this point onwards. I rolled over, trying to escape from the truth. Maybe they would understand,

22

but I hadn't been there very long. Who knew how they would react?

I could hear Georgina finishing in the shower, so I grabbed my toiletries and towel. I would jump straight in when I heard her go back into her room. I realised that my room on the ward, with its own shower, was technically a better room. I smiled to myself at the irony. After that, the morning continued like normal. As if nothing out of the ordinary had happened at all. It was a warm day, but not as hot as it had been. Summer was starting to fade away and before long it would give way to autumn.

Georgina gave me a lift as planned and we sat in silence most of the way there. The mornings were different to when we usually spent time together, we were sleepy and easily annoyed each other. She pulled up by the station, and I turned to her and smiled.

"Thanks hun, have a good day," I said.

"You too babes, good luck," she replied.

Good luck. Yes, I guess I would need it. I walked up to the office I had been working at for just under two months. Everyone seemed lovely and I was settling in well. I was normally one of the first in to work, so I put a fresh pot of coffee on and grabbed some cereal from my desk drawer. I would normally eat my breakfast at work whilst catching up on my emails. I had so much to catch up on, it was almost overwhelming. As my head was still all over the place I decided to take it slow and scroll through to read the important ones first.

My boss walked in not long after me. Her name was Marie and she was in her late forties. Marie was French and married to a Chinese guy nearly twenty years younger than her. Together they had the most beautiful baby boy. Pictures of him were scattered all over Marie's desk. She was a nice enough boss, but strict when it came to silly mistakes. I'd always had good attention to detail, so we got on fairly well. I felt I could trust her and hoped one day to be her friend. She was wearing barely anything, as she got hot very easily. I looked ridiculous compared to her with my very formal outfit.

"Morning," she said, with a sleepy smile on her face, iced coffee in hand.

"Morning!"

"Good holiday?"

"Yeah, lovely thanks. Did I miss anything important?"

"Oh no, nothing much. Natalie got promoted to Head of Communications, but nothing much other than that. You've met Natalie right? The black girl?" Marie said.

"Yes..." I said, still slightly taken aback by how my boss spoke about people. How would she describe me? "We've been out drinking a couple times together."

"Oh, nice. We should all go some time."

"That would be lovely!" I smiled. She sat at her desk. I knew Monday mornings were not very busy at our office, so I decided that I would see if we could talk at some point today. "Marie, at some point today, would you be available for a quick chat?" I said as politely as I could.

"Of course, why? What's up? You're not thinking of leaving us are you? Don't! We love you here, you're better than Ali and he's been here for years!"

"Oh no, it's nothing like that, just something I want to discuss. It's not important at all."

"Oh, right. Ok. Everything ok though?"

"Yes, honestly. All is good." I started to feel nervous, so turned back to my emails and started to eat my breakfast again. I would work extra hard today and try not to think about things too much.

* * *

Luckily, as I had to spend so much time catching up from the week I had off, the morning seemed to go a lot faster than it normally did. Before long it was 2 p.m. and Marie called me into the conference room. She had bought another iced coffee and treated me to one too. I was so touched by her kindness. I brought my pen and notepad into the conference room, and put them down on the table next to me. I was sweating from the heat, but I'm sure it also had something to do with my nerves.

"So what is it you wanted to talk about?" Marie asked abruptly. "You sure you aren't going anywhere?"

"No, it's something else. It's something personal actually, some stuff in my head that I've always known I needed to sort out..." I had planned how I was going to tell her everything in my notes, but I was suddenly too nervous to be able to read them. My head went blank and all I could think about was the week I had spent in hospital. Obviously I wasn't about to tell her that! I wasn't going to tell anyone about how I took a fake holiday, had attempted to commit suicide, and had been in a mental ward. I wasn't going to tell her how I started crying so loudly at the hospital that they had to move me to a different area. Nor was I going to admit that I broke down and had a small fit because of what one of the other patients called me.

"Ok, spit it out then." She brought my focus back and I looked up from my notes.

I continued to explain my situation to her and what would happen from now on. I remained as positive as possible, and wherever I could, I tried to make it clear that I loved my job, and wanted to stay here long term. That much was true, I really did like my job. It was an office made up mostly of women, each one strong and independent. I felt I could be myself and would hopefully grow within the company. Having a female boss was the best thing for me, as male bosses always intimidated me.

"I see." Marie said, after I had finished explaining everything.

It suddenly went very quiet. Marie remained very still, and I looked down at my notes.

"I'm not sure how my manager will react, if I'm honest. They might not want to continue your contract. I would start looking for other work."

"Excuse me?"

"I'm sorry, but if I were you I would start looking for other work."

I couldn't believe my ears. What did she just say? Did she... what? I didn't understand. Everything around me went dark and I felt like I was dreaming. Surely that was discrimination. Surely that was illegal.

"Are you even allowed to say that?"

"Well your probation hasn't finished yet, I doubt they will carry you on." She said sternly.

"Are you serious? Why? I haven't done anything wrong, I'm only saying about..." I stopped. There was no point. I was so shocked that I would end up shouting at her and get myself fired on the spot. Instead I just stared at her cruel hard face for a moment, and in utter shock grabbed my notepad and pen. Then I thought to myself, what the hell am I doing? She can have her job. And I walked over to the bin and dropped the notepad and pen straight in it. She remained as still as a rock. The office could see through the glass door that my face had turned completely white and that something was very wrong. Avoiding their eyes I stormed back to my desk but didn't sit down. I grabbed my bag, wiped a tear from my eye and headed for the door. A couple of my colleagues stood up to see what was wrong, but most of them just sat there awkwardly.

I was practically running for the lift. More tears were starting to blur my vision, and my stomach was starting to cramp. I couldn't breathe. Did that really just happen? Did she really just tell me to look for other work because I'm... I couldn't believe it. I'm sure that was illegal. How could she do that? Only ten minutes ago she was asking me to stay. Was what I wanted to do for myself, for my own personal well-being really that terrible? It was as if I had told her I had killed someone or something! I felt violated and physically sick. A feeling of rage swept over me like a wave of hot air.

After leaving the office in disbelief, I walked straight into the nearest pub and ordered a glass of white wine. It was only 2:30 p.m. but there were already other office workers drinking in there too, so I didn't care. After what just happened, I didn't care at all. The cute bartender asked if I was ok. His muscles were bulging out of his top, and I suddenly felt shy having his eyes on me.

"Rough day?" He asked, smiling sweetly.

"I just walked out of my office. I think I just quit my job." I blurted out. He was handsome and I was lonely. I clearly wasn't his type, but at that particular moment I didn't care.

"Oh, fuck, really? Then this one is on the house." He put the card machine away, as I was about to put my card in it. He nodded intently at me and went on to a different customer. Two old men were sipping beers a couple of feet away from me.

Did that bartender just say "fuck"? I giggled to myself in disbelief.

I picked up the free glass of wine and took a long sip. It made me feel slightly sick this early in the day, but I had eaten earlier at lunch so I was confident that it wouldn't get me drunk. What was I going to do? What was I actually going to do? I was now jobless. What a bitch! How could she flip so quickly like that?

After a quarter of the glass I decided I needed to change things there and then. I needed to sort out the shit that was going on in my head as soon as possible. I decided that maybe a hair cut would be a good start. Lots of people in films get their hair cut when they break up or something drastic. I could do that. I put my hand through my hair and wondered if it would look ok. Yes. That's what I would do – I would cut my hair into a pixie cut. That would help. I would feel better. I needed a change. Yes. I stood up. Yes.

I downed the rest of the wine, which made me gag slightly, and left the pub. As I walked out into the sunlight it felt like the clouds had moved out of the way for me. I looked up and the blue sky was so lovely that I paused for a moment. It really was beautiful. I decided that I would take it as a sign. This was going to be a good thing – I would make it a good thing. I was all about change now anyway. Perhaps a new career was exactly what I needed?

The hair salon nearest to my office was probably too expensive for me, as I worked in the centre of London. So I decided to make my way home to Camden first and find one around there. I had the rest of the day, so I was in no rush. When I got off the tube I noticed a small independent salon, which didn't look busy at all.

I walked in. The staff all looked at me and smiled.

"Hello there, do you have an appointment?" One of the shorter members of staff squeaked at me. Her voice was so high-pitched that I could barely hear her. She had far too much blusher on and was chewing gum. Lovely.

"Erm, no. No appointment. I was wondering if you could cut my hair into a pixie cut actually..."

"A what? A pixie cut? Really? Are you sure?" She looked confused.

"Yes please, I need a change. Can I also dye it red?" Where did that come from? Red!?

"Red? Wow, you really do want a change! Ok... let's see what we can do..." She looked hesitant, but kind of excited.

She waved me over to an empty seat, and I was forced to stare at myself in the mirror. I looked back at myself. I was so tall that she had to adjust the height of the seat to reach me. Or she was too short – I couldn't tell. We talked about casual stuff at first, but then I told her about my work. I told her everything – about my boss Marie, about my flatmate Georgina, about being in hospital. Everything. It all fell out like a waterfall of words. It gushed out into the empty room. The other staff had gone out to smoke, or were out the back on their breaks. It was just me, this short girl and all her blusher. She listened to my every word and nodded along slowly. I didn't think she would be so understanding, but she was.

"Well good for you babes, it sounds like that place was a shitty place to work anyway! They totally don't deserve you." She was cutting as she talked, and I could see my hair falling to the floor. There wasn't as much of it on the floor as I had expected. Before long it was done, and I looked into the mirror again. She hadn't dyed it red yet, but I could already see a difference. It looked trendy and sexy. I loved it. I had never had a hairstyle like this – it was exactly the change I needed.

"Do you like it?" She asked. She was more nervous than I was.

"I... I love it! Thank you so, so much!" I meant it. I really was happy. I had almost forgotten about the terrible day it had been.

"Ok darling, I'm going to go and mix the dye then – sit tight, I won't be long."

When we were finished, I paid her a generous tip. As I strutted out into the cleansing sunshine, I felt like Beyoncé in her spotlight. I felt fresh and unbreakable. Fuck Marie. Fuck that job. I would find something else. I would be fine – it was all about the future for me. I felt a tingle in my hands and a burst of energy coursing through my body. The sunshine was filling me up and burning away the anxiety and fear. Everything was going to be ok. I could feel it.

Prince Hikaru was Queen Fubuki's true love. He was Prince rather than King because even after their handfasting, his title could not be superior to hers. He was summoned to the Palace of Crystal the day after what would be known as the Assassination on Peace. The innocent villager in the crowd of the Songshow had been poisoned without a single soul noticing. Not even the great mage herself. The entire nation was mortified and chaos spread across the land. For a place that had only ever known peace, the idea that someone could die a painful death was a haunting notion.

The braver of those in Macha Land tried to go about their lives as normal. The markets just East of the Main Stage were still thriving, but they were no longer filled with rich velvets and silks, rather potions for health and good fortune. Rune readers swarmed the streets, exploiting the turmoil for their own personal gain. High priestesses from the Coven of Rosemary, who usually gathered just South of the Ice Mountain, headed to the capital to cast as many spells for protection as their energy pools would allow.

However, most of the people of the nation decided to hide within their homes and dared not leave. The Queen tried to ensure that enough food and water was delivered to everyone, so that they could last the Winter. She would organise it herself if she had to, bargaining with the farmers and markets so they would deliver to her people. In the Southern regions, just North of the Southern Beaches, many of the animals and astral beings found the stirring activity so off-putting that they migrated further South. The merpeople were already as far South as they could go, since they couldn't cope with the icy climate of the North. The Ice Mountain stood tall as it did each Winter. It seemed to watch over everything.

Prince Hikaru was at the market when he felt the Queen summon him. He heard her voice as if she was standing right next to him.

Come, my love. I need you.

He put down the jewel encrusted yew bow that he had been inspecting, and turned to face the Palace. It was miles and miles to the North, but it could still be seen sparkling in the distance. However, it was nothing compared to the Main Stage, which was much closer to Hikaru, just a short walk West. The Main Stage was so bright that it could be seen from every part of Macha Land. Hikaru assumed that that must have been the reason the Queen had created it entirely from crystal.

The wind was harsh and it felt like it would go right through him were it not for the brown fur cloak he had wrapped around himself. The cloak was made from the pelt of a magnificently large fox that Hikaru had hunted several moons back. He had been in the woods not far from the market, when he heard a small child screaming in the distance. After running to the child's aid, he saw paw prints so large that he could fit his whole forearm inside them. He managed to save the small boy, who was only dressed in rags, and took the feral fox down too. The fox would have eaten the boy whole had it not been for the Prince. Nonetheless, Hikaru felt shame for what he had done. The fox should not have died on that day. He made the boy apologise for wandering so far into the woods and disrupting the creatures. To ensure that the fox's death had not been in vain, he spent half a day skinning it for its fur, took the meat to the village close by and the woodland elves thanked the Goddess for it. Then he burnt the corpse to prevent it rotting. Hikaru finished by making two cloaks, one for himself and one for the boy. The young boy never went walking in the woods again.

Hikaru, come to me...

Prince Hikaru snapped out of his day dream and made his way to the market gates. The brown cloak dragged behind him on the cold, muddy floor. Underneath this, Hikaru wore simple clothes. He had never liked the weight of chainmail and found leather too binding. He was a warrior of speed, and preferred to be able to move swiftly around his enemy. To keep warm, he wore several layers of linen, but it still allowed his skin to breathe, and let his body move as he needed it to. He owned a small leather bag that he tied to his belt, and a pair of leather boots. That was all he needed.

His weapon of choice today was a small dagger made entirely of silver and frozen mercury – a gift from the Queen herself. The metal had been forged with molten silver and liquid mercury, tempered gently and then enchanted with ice by one of the magi from the Coven of Rosemary, deep in the heart of the Ice Mountain. Since the Ice Mountain only existed in Winter, it was therefore named 'Winter's Dagger'. Once mercury is frozen, it is sharper than any other metal known to man and it also glistens slightly, which can help to distract the enemy.

The path to the Queen's Palace was directly North of the Main Stage, so he decided to head in that direction. Then suddenly, before he had even reached the market gates, he could feel himself getting lighter. He felt weightless and aery. A white light blinded him and the surrounding villagers stared in amazement. He took a deep breath and let himself disappear into the void. The Queen must be feeling impatient today.

"I called you several times, my Prince. Why did you not answer? I was worried you were hurt." He heard her say before the white light around him had faded.

"My Queen..." His voice was still trembling from the teleportation spell. "I was on my way to you. You seem more agitated than usual. Please, you must be calm." She could feel the anxiety leaving her tense body the second she heard his voice, and a natural smile appeared on her face. It was her first smile since the Assassination on Peace. "Come here," he gestured playfully.

She got up from her crystal chair that was draped in crimson velvet and dove into his outstretched arms. He held her tightly, and ran his thumb over her right cheek.

"I'm scared Hikaru. I have no idea what is happening. If I don't even know what is happening, how can I presume to stop it?" She just wanted him to comfort her. She didn't really expect an answer.

"Let's go over the facts. The Coven of Rosemary is sure it was poison, yes?" Hikaru pulled away from her slightly.

"Yes... the strongest they have ever known. His body fell to pieces in minutes."

"If it was poison, then it must be something or someone that came into contact with him. There might be something that wants to harm your people." Hikaru was deep in thought. His face was brooding and tense. He gently let her go from his embrace altogether. With one hand stroking his chin, he began to pace the room. The warmth inside the Palace started to spread to him, so he removed his cloak and dropped it over the chair that the Queen was sitting on as he paced the room. He turned to her, and looked deep into her eyes. "Did you notice anything else, anything at all that we could go on?"

"No, nothing," lied the Queen. She had seen that black figure when she was flying in the sky, but she didn't want to admit that to Hikaru. He would want to go in search of whatever it was and she wanted him by her side.

"Don't lie to me, my Queen. You know full well that I can tell when you're lying to me." He smiled at her. His eyes were full of love.

"Fine, but you have to promise me you will not leave suddenly and pursue it," she demanded. She was a Queen, even to Hikaru. If she wanted him to stay with her, then he would have to stay.

"I promise to obey, my Queen. Now what was it? Go after what?" It was her safety that was at stake, despite neither of them wanting to admit it. An attack on her people was an attack on her.

"When I transformed into the Phoenix, I saw a blackish figure in the distance. It looked blurry, but it was large." The Queen explained it all, as she saw it in her mind's eye.

"I see. And you think it's connected?"

"I do. It must be. It was standing atop the Ice Mountain. Calm, but watchful. That's what it felt like, anyway."

The Queen felt another pang of fear and walked out onto the balcony of her sleeping quarters. She could see the entire island from her balcony, the Main Stage, the Windy Planes and even the Southern beaches. Behind her towered the Palace made entirely of crystal. It was shaped like a cone, with a few rooms on the outer edges of it. Through the only door of the Palace, to the right, was a staircase with no bannister that curved along the back wall and up to the second level. On the second level were her sleeping quarters, but they were not sectioned off by any doors or walls. Her bed was a simple dip in the floor, filled with velvet cushions and satin sheets. Directly beneath that, and left of the entrance was a circular room that she would often be found meditating in. She had no need for cooking quarters, or other such rooms. The Palace crept hundreds of feet into the clouds, tapering from the base. The Veil of Warmth was cast from the very top of the Palace, and covered the island for thousands of miles South, and a short distance North.

Within this glorious cave of crystal, the Queen and her Prince were deep in thought as to how to stop whatever threatened their ever peaceful realm. They were both tall and slim, and had thin, dark eyes. They could be mistaken for elves, were they not the two most recognised people in this world, and known to be but human.

"My Queen. What would you have me do? I will follow your instructions, as always."

"That's precisely the problem, Hikaru. I don't know how to instruct you." She turned away from the balcony and looked at him. "That poor, innocent man died... Why, Hikaru, why?" Tears began to fill her eyes. Her fear got the better of her and she started to ache all over. Hikaru ran to her, and placed his hands on her lower back to steady her.

"Fubuki, be strong my love." His voice was calm, but powerful. To her, his words were like medicine. She had to find her strength, and find whoever was responsible for the death of the innocent villager.

Deep within her she could feel something change. She could feel her fear transform into fury. She was the Queen. She was one of the strongest mages in Macha Land. It had always been that way. She could summon red lightning with her hands and turn into a flaming red Phoenix.

"Hikaru, you're right. What are we doing here? Why are we wasting time? I am Fubuki. Queen Fubuki. I will find whoever did this, and stop them. I will avenge his life, as it is only I who can do so." Queen Fubuki's long, straight, dark hair began to move as a gentle wind filled the Palace. She stood on her balcony, her eyes drifting over her lands. Hikaru could feel her magick grow stronger with every breath. This is the Queen he knew. This is the woman he loved.

* * *

It took the rest of the evening to prepare everything. She sent Prince Hikaru to the markets in search of supplies – purple candles, various herbs, raven feathers, milk, three silver coins, a small, pointed

Amethyst crystal on a chain, a purple ribbon, a well-drawn map of the island and the purest salt he could find. Meanwhile, Queen Fubuki was with the Coven of Rosemary, in the magi's tower. She was there to discuss her spell. The Coven of Rosemary would want to know what form the spell would take.

Once everything was set, both Prince Hikaru and Queen Fubuki met each other back at the Palace. However, they didn't enter it. Instead, Hikaru set down the supplies on the floor just in front of the entrance. Fubuki stood calmly for a moment, on the damp grass, to take in the cool Winter's air. Once all ten candles were set in a complete Circle and the salt was scattered around to purify the area, Hikaru walked back to stand next to the Palace door. Queen Fubuki closed her eyes, and walked into the centre of the Circle. Everything was placed perfectly around her. All she had to focus on, was what came next. The Circle allowed her plenty of room to move if she had to. For now she stood very still, with her feet at shoulder width apart and her hands by her side.

She wore ribbons in her hair to tie it back – they were the same shade of purple as her candles. She chose a simple, black silk gown that embraced her body but still flared out from her waist. A silver belt was wrapped tightly around her hips. The thin, black material of her dress was almost see-through and blew gently in the winds.

Then she began.

"Oshiete, Oshiete, Oshiete kudasai..." She chanted in a deep and bold voice the words of the Goddess. It seemed to fill the entire sky. Birds in the trees began to sing back at her. Wolves in the forest howled. Merpeople sang all the way in the South. The night turned darker and the winds turned colder. Queen Fubuki was using her magick. The entire realm could sense it when Queen Fubuki cast a spell. The air became thick with anticipation and excitement.

"…Oshiete kudasai…"

She felt herself lifting off the ground. Her arms floated up and she forced them in front of her, into an orb shape. She broke her chant.

"Reveal who did this!" She screamed. Purple lightning flashed in the distance, far beyond the island she was on, and thunder roared across the oceans towards the South West. Red orbs of lights appeared between her hands and red sparks of electricity ran up and down her arms. Her hair broke free from the tightly fastened ribbons as the winds blew upwards. Great beams of purple light shined through her as the candles surrounding her burst into flames as tall as she was. The crystal on the floor beneath her started to shake and the map of the island blew upwards. It caught alight in the flames of one of the surrounding candles and circled around the Queen. It sparkled with energy and the orb between Fubuki's hands grew larger and stronger. Eventually, the map was drawn into her orb of power and within that moment, a light, so bright it forced Hikaru to look away, exploded from her hands and shined outwards all around her.

The Palace of Crystal absorbed the light and channelled it through the tall crystal ceiling. It reached the top of the tower and burst outwards across the sky. Within moments, the magnificent purple light enveloped the entire island. The evil creature that had poisoned the innocent in the crowd would be struck by a lightning bolt of pure purple energy. Queen Fubuki would then know where to look for the culprit. She would get her revenge, and restore peace to the realm as swiftly as it had been taken.

She waited. Her feet had landed softly back on the cold grass. Her energy began to drain from her as she grounded herself. Her jet black hair fell down behind her back and all ten candles went out simultaneously in a wisp of smoke. Hikaru watched the purple sky, as did Fubuki. They waited. Yet nothing happened. No signs. No lightning. Nothing. Not even a ripple in the purple bubble that she had cast. Had it failed? Surely not, her spells always worked.

"My Prince. No sign to guide the way... there can be only one explanation for this." She said quietly to her lover.

"The enemy we seek must not be on this island."

"Exactly. They must be on the small island, miles and miles from here." For the first time in the conversation she looked back to Hikaru. She didn't move her body, only her head. She stared at him, filled with both rage and confusion. "The abandoned island to the South West has been a lifeless wasteland for centuries, so they must be on Volcano Island." Queen Fubuki spoke fiercely, but still didn't move her body.

"Yes, my Queen." The prince bowed his head and closed his eyes.

"I release this Circle," shouted the Queen into the purple night's sky. Her voice hit the Ice Mountain and echoed into the distance. She heard ice hit snow powerfully as it fell from high above the ground. Birds took flight from the trees, and the people of the villages looked to the skies to watch the spectacle that was about to occur.

The purple light that shined across Macha Land started to shimmer, and then burst into a million tiny sparks in the sky. The stars appeared to be exploding. The energy was so strong that the entire realm felt alive with power. Whoever had poisoned the innocent villager, wherever they may be, would surely see it too.

"Prince Hikaru... Go to the docks by the Bridge Over the River. Gather the Four Guardians and as skilled a crew as you require. You shall be sailing to the Volcano Island on the morrow. Take whatever ship you wish. I will take to the skies and get there first. Make what preparations you need immediately. We leave at dawn." The Queen's anger made her feel strong and her spell made her feel yet more powerful.

"Yes, my Queen. As you command." And with that, Prince Hikaru walked over to her and kissed her on the lips. She fell into his embrace and rested her face on his hard shoulders. He wrapped his cloak around her cold and shivering body and they stood there together for what felt like eternity.

"What do you mean you quit your job?" My Mum was shouting so loudly down the phone I had to move it away from my ear.

"You don't understand, it just wasn't going to work out. It's fine, honestly. I will find another job as soon as I can." I tried to sound convincing. I was still in bed at 11 a.m. on a Tuesday. I had some new butterfly pyjamas on, and an instant coffee on the bedside cabinet to my left. Georgina had gone to work and told me to come and meet her for lunch if I needed some company.

"No, *you* don't understand. It's not going to be easy to find a job in your... condition." My mum fell silent.

"Mum, it's not like I'm terminally ill. Plenty of people in my *condition* can find work just fine, thank you. Look, I have to go. I need to sort out my CV, ok?" I was too hurt to talk to her. How could she talk down to me like that? I told my parents about my so-called "condition" the night I left the hospital. Obviously I didn't tell them about the mental health hospital itself. No way.

"Ok, fine. Just promise me you'll go to the job centre today. I worry about you B." She never called me Beam. Only B.

"I will. I promise." I said, genuinely meaning it.

"Bye. Take care of yourself, ok?"

"Yes mum, I will. Love you."

"Love you too."

I hung up. The phone fell from my hands to the bed. I sipped the coffee and curled up in my new pyjamas. They looked so pretty. I loved them. Butterflies were my new favourite thing. I decided that I would go to the job centre, explain everything, and try to get a step closer to sorting my life out.

The afternoon was more humid than the day before, which made it even harder to pick what to wear.

I didn't want to wear anything too formal and bulky, but I didn't have many clothes to choose from. I needed to wear a long top and formal trousers but I decided against a suit jacket. All I had were my smart shoes, but I hated how clunky they looked. It all seemed too big and unflattering. I went with a simple, slim fit, white shirt and plain, black trousers. My new red hair would be enough colour. It was 12 p.m. by the time I was ready. Georgina was texting me, but I was so focused on going to the job centre that I ignored her. I would see her tonight anyway.

I stepped out into the street, and it was like living somewhere completely different. Mums walked along happily with their pushchairs. Old ladies sat patiently at the bus stop. Buses came and went with only four passengers on them. It was nothing like I was used to. This wasn't the Camden I knew. Normally, I left at rush hour and came home at rush hour. I preferred this new London.

The job centre was in the scariest part of town. Ordinarily, I would be scared to even drive past there. But I had no choice. If anything happened to me, I could ring Georgina and she would help. I was really glad to have her as a friend. I should have texted her back sooner. The sun was blazing down on me and I pulled my phone out to reply to her text from a couple of hours ago. A group of young boys hanging out outside the job centre started looking at me, pointing and even laughing. I told myself that it was my new red hair and ignored them. It was midday – I was perfectly safe. Right?

After walking into the building, I finished texting Georgina and put my phone away. I could feel everyone's eyes on me. It was horrible. I already wanted to be back home with a nice coffee and my butterfly pyjamas on. No. I had to be strong. I looked around me. People were everywhere. I realised I was the only one wearing anything resembling formal attire, including the staff, who had started to notice me too. Did I stand out that much? It was so fucking horrible. I felt like a clown.

"Hi there, can I help you?" One of the receptionists called out to me.

"Yes, hello there. I recently decided to terminate my contract at work, and am seeking employment elsewhere." Ok, maybe I didn't need to talk like I was on the Apprentice, but first impressions were everything. I remembered to smile, and make eye contact, but tried to not overdo it.

"Of course, will you be applying for jobseeker's allowance too?"

"Do you think I will need to?"

"It's up to you. Probably not if you plan to be working straight away, but it could take time for you to find the right position." The woman was polite, but cold. Her blonde hair was tied back in a ponytail and she was wearing casual clothes.

"I see, ok. Then yes, please." It seemed like a sensible idea, although I didn't want to be out of work for a long time. The receptionist instructed me to go to the 3rd floor and wait to be seen. I smiled politely and made my way to the lift. Various sets of eyes seemed to be fixed on me, and I could feel them burning into my back. I was the elephant in the room. A part of me wanted to turn around and sarcastically wave goodbye to everyone as I left. It was like I was some kind of freak.

As I was waiting for the lift, I could see a large dog outside, in a small park. There was no one around, and it was tied to a bench. I assumed the dog's owner had only left for a moment. The dog cocked his leg and started to urinate. I could see him doing it very clearly. I saw absolutely everything. I forced myself to look away from the poor, lonely dog and hoped his owner would return soon. The lift to the 3rd floor was empty and dark, but I had no choice but to take it. Like the dog, I was stuck. Trapped. Alone.

I stepped inside the lift, the doors closed and I was surrounded by mirrors. Mirrors couldn't lie. They didn't know how. It made me think about him. If he were here now, what would he have done? Would he have done anything differently? Would he even have found himself in a place like this? I doubted it. He was always such a strong, hard-working person. Or at least he acted like it. That was all he ever did... act. He was so false. So fake. The mirrors showed only the truth. Or did they lie to me too? Was what I saw in the mirrors inside this lift a lie? They didn't reflect the real me, and they wouldn't have reflected the real him either. It was such a contradiction. Everything was.

My head was starting to ache. Time seemed to go slowly as the lift ascended higher. Was I crazy? No. The doctors wouldn't have let me go if I was. Thousands of people went through what I was going through. I couldn't be crazy. So what, then? Unlucky? Yes... that made more sense. I was unlucky. I thought about him again. Actually, if anyone was unlucky, it was him. Not me. Him.

The 3rd floor was an interesting place. Young boys, clearly on drugs, were sat on uncomfortable chairs, waiting to be seen. Mums sat with children in their arms, whilst being told "the money will be with you in due course". When I walked out of the lift, I could feel the stares again. It must have been the red hair. Yes, it was the red hair, I had decided. I sat and waited too, ignoring the people around me, and looked over my notes. In order to be taken seriously, I made sure to have what I wanted to say written down. This only drew more attention to me. After a few minutes, it was finally my time to be seen.

I walked over to the desk. The whole floor was an open plan office, so I could still see the area where I had just been sitting. To the right, the wall of windows let the rays of sun through, which meant the poor staff members closest to the window were in constant contact with the heat. I didn't envy them. The man sitting at the desk in front of me was in his thirties. He seemed underweight, wore a pink cardigan and had highlights in his hair. When he saw me, his eyes widened a little.

"Hello... please, take a seat." His voice was soft and slightly camp. I didn't want to assume, but I was almost certain that he was gay. In a way, I was relieved. Straight men always intimidated me.

"Hello. Thank you very much for seeing me today."

"You're welcome. Can I take your form from you please?" I handed him the form that I had downloaded from the internet, and filled out before I came. It went into incredible detail about my personal life, work history and general health. I could imagine how that would annoy most people, having to write something so degrading, but I didn't mind. I was here to find work, and get help.

"Of course, here it is. You can see my name on the front, but please call me Beam. Everyone calls me Beam."

"Beam... that's an interesting nickname. What does it mean?"

"Beam, as in a beam of light, I guess."

"Aww, that's cute. Ok then, Beam, how can I help you today?"

"Well, I guess I should just explain everything to you, right?" I said, sounding slightly nervous. "I am looking for a new job, after basically getting fired from my old one for no real reason. Well, I recently came out of hospital because I tried to kill myself last week. It was a last resort from... well... you can see on my record." I pointed to the place where it was written out and the man nodded slowly. "I was told to leave my job because they wouldn't renew my contract after finding out everything, so I am here to look for work at a place that will take me." I couldn't stop talking. "I studied business at college, always got good grades, which you can see on my CV here." I handed him my CV and work experience documents. "I hope to find work as soon as I can, but if that doesn't seem likely, then I would also like to apply for jobseeker's allowance." I finished and was almost out of breath.

"Ok! That's a lot of information! It's nice to see someone taking this so seriously though. I wish everyone else would. So what we are going to do is put you forward for jobseeker's allowance, just in case you don't find work. It will take a couple of weeks for you to get any money in your account anyway, so it's best to get this process started early."

"Ok, sure." *Why would it be difficult for me to find work?* I thought to myself. *Isn't he going to help me find something?*

"Also, I'm going to need you to keep this booklet updated with all of your job hunting activities. You can also do it online by following this link. It will record what you apply for and give you suggestions as well."

"Sure – no problem." I took the booklet, it seemed easy enough to fill in.

"I will need to see you once a week, so we can catch up on your progress. By the sounds of things, you know what you want, so hopefully I won't be seeing you for very long!"

"No... I... I guess not. Do you have any work placement suggestions now that I can look into? I'm eager to find work straightaway."

"Well, it might take a bit longer for someone like you, if I'm honest." Ouch, there it was. I saw his eyes glance at the details on my forms. "It's a shame though, you really do seem eager to work." He looked at me with a sad face. He seemed to be pitying me.

"Please, is there nothing I can do now?" I begged. Why on earth was I begging?

"I do have some customer service roles that you can apply for straight away. You seem like a smiley person. Why don't you go for one of those?"

Customer service, I guess it did relate to business. I did love to smile, but being in the public eye was a slightly scary idea at this point. I started to remember my mum earlier on the phone. Then I started to panic – what if I never found anything? Maybe I should just take the first thing that comes up, and if something better came up later on, then I could take that then. Yes, that's what I would do. I had no time to lose.

"Ok, I will take a look. Can I apply for one now, if I see one I like?"

"Yes of course, I can set you up on the system now and apply with you if you want." He seemed sincere. I wanted to impress him. At that moment, I felt like life was a competition, and I wasn't going to let my misfortunes hold me back anymore. I was done with that. I had to be strong, I had to prove that I was normal.

We spent the next hour setting up my Jobcentre Plus account, and applying for three of the customer service roles that were available straight away. The guy annoyed me a bit when he told me I was unlikely to get an office job with hair like mine – but then again, he did have a point. Was it reckless of me to dye it red? Maybe. But I liked it, and I was all about being myself at the moment.

One of the three positions was in a restaurant in Central London. The hours were later than I was used to, but meals were included. The job centre employee had sent that application first, and we were in the middle of typing out the second when the phone rang.

"Hello, Jobcentre Plus, how can I help?"

I couldn't hear the other side of the conversation.

"Oh really, that's great." He looked straight at me. "Sure, yes, I can pass you over now if you want?" He suddenly pressed a button and forced the phone in my direction.

"Who is it?" I asked confused.

"It's the manager of the restaurant you just applied for. He saw your application and just wants a quick chat." The guy said, he almost seemed excited for me.

"Oh, right. Wow, that's good!" I was shocked at how fast this was all going, although I had been there for nearly two hours now. No one else was waiting to be seen anymore.

"Just introduce yourself, and be natural. They must be interested if they rang straight away."

"Ok, sure. I'm ready." The guy pushed the button to take the call off hold. The bustling sound of staff running around and hot food sizzling started bursting through the phone.

"Hello? Is that... Beam? My name's Paul, nice to meet you."

"Yes, hello! Thank you very much for getting back to me so quickly."

"No problem! Thanks for sending over your CV." He seemed energetic, friendly and casual. "So, I see you studied business then. Any customer service experience?"

"Well, although it wasn't face to face, I did deal with client complaints at the office I worked at."

"Oh, ok, that's good. Why did you leave your office job, can I ask?"

"I was asked to leave actually. Because of how I'm..." What do I say? The truth? If he read through my profile I guess he must have seen?

"Don't worry, we don't judge anyone here. We are a real "be yourself" bunch. Very relaxed." It was like he read my mind. He seemed so sweet and kind. It would be refreshing to work with someone that was relaxed. Maybe this could be part of the 'new me'?

"That sounds great! Thanks for being so understanding"

"It's £7 an hour, 20 hours minimum a week. Meals on the job. Uniform is all black. How does that sound?" He spoke so fast I could barely understand him. The noise in the background didn't help. The guy behind the job centre desk seemed surprisingly happy for me. He was sipping a cup of tea that another member of staff had just brought him. His mug had a picture of a topless man on it. I held in a laugh. How cute.

"Fantastic, that all sounds perfect."

"All right, good." He seemed distracted, as if the restaurant suddenly needed his attention. "Can you come in tomorrow night for a trial shift? Say 5 p.m.?"

"Yes, of course! All black, right?"

"All black, yes. See you then, Beam." He was so kind to me – I felt like I didn't deserve it. The phone line went dead immediately after. He really was busy.

"I hope I made a good impression. I'm going in tomorrow for a trial shift."

"That's great news! You've got something to fill in your booklet already then! Well, go home, practice your smile, and let me know how it goes. Don't worry if you don't get it, as it's still very early days." He brought me back down to earth with that last comment. I shouldn't get my hopes up – it was the first place I'd applied too. But I couldn't help but feel a little bit confident, it seemed like a relaxed environment. Maybe it was exactly what I needed. The manager seemed really understanding. I thought back to when I was in hospital. I would never have imagined that I would be here now, with red hair, applying to work in a restaurant. My life was changing rapidly, but I felt like it was for the better. I wanted to believe it was for the better.

It didn't matter what was going on in my head if I was working at a restaurant. It didn't matter about my past, or my future. All I had to do was smile, and serve the customers. It would be easy. Yes, it wasn't great money, but if something better came along I would take it then. I had nothing to lose. Maybe I would really find myself – my new self.

That night I snuggled into bed with my new butterfly pyjamas on, after making me and Georgina a nice spaghetti Bolognese. I thought about my dreams and how crazy they had been getting. I thought about what the psychoanalysts had said in the mental hospital. I thought about the night I tried to kill myself. I never wanted to feel like that again. My eyes felt heavy, and the heat was closing in on me. I rolled over and let myself fall into a deep sleep, only to dream of her again.

The Bridge was built over the widest part of the river that reached into the centre of Macha Land, and acted like a gate to the mouth of the island. It was mainly built from bricks and was decorated with wooden planks. The Veil of Warmth came to a cold end this far West of the island, so the Bridge was covered in blankets of powdered snow. Shivering villagers and creatures from the River had come to wish Queen Fubuki and Prince Hikaru farewell. Many more from throughout the vast island would also have come to catch a glimpse of the glorious Queen, had it not been for the biting cold.

Prince Hikaru had chosen a ship and gathered enough men and women to sail it. Also aboard the small but steady ship were Queen Fubuki's Four Guardians, each in their dark red and black armour. Queen Fubuki had lent Prince Hikaru her beloved horse for the journey as well. The horse, named Kaze, was such dark black that he couldn't be easily seen after dusk. Hikaru stroked the steed's long black mane, and fed him a carrot from one of those stockpiled for the voyage. Kaze chewed merrily and let Hikaru ruffle his mane.

The sun was only just rising. Queen Fubuki could be seen flying in the icy sky. She was once again in her Phoenix form, and large icicles danced around her like wilting flowers as they fell from the sky above her. Prince Hikaru stopped stroking Kaze, and in awe of his beautiful Queen, couldn't help but stare up at her. He knew that it was no accident that the innocent man had been poisoned. It was murder. He knew that whatever was happening to Macha Land was dangerous. He had to protect her. He had to be there for her. He promised himself, as she blazed across the sky like a comet, that he would die for her if he had to.

From high above her Prince, Queen Fubuki felt like the Goddess herself. Her tail was formed of two long, vine-like parts, with tufts of feathers at the end.

They were burning hot with fire. Her wings were bright red, with orange and yellow tints in the centre. Her beak was sharp. Her feathers looked like fiery water, as they danced in the wind. As the Phoenix, she felt unstoppable. She was a symbol of strength, of rebirth, of femininity.

When she reached the Bridge Over the River, she landed gracefully at the very summit of the arching brickwork. Prince Hikaru was almost directly underneath her, on the ship, still by Kaze's side. The crowds that had gathered cheered as the steam rose from the snow that had once lain peacefully on the path where Fubuki now rested.

"Our Queen!" They roared.

"Queen Fubuki!"

"Blessed be!"

Amongst the screams, a myriad of sounds could be heard. The howl of wolves, the harmonious hum of the few merpeople still living in the River and even the cluck of roosters in the distance. The morning dew soaked the shoes of many villagers as they came to wish their Queen a safe journey. A High Priestess was also there with a large bundle of sage. She lit the end and clouds of smoke drifted from the shore and circled the ship. As the smoke rose up beyond the ship, Queen Fubuki was also enveloped, and it filled the fires of her body with great strength.

And yet, deep down, Fubuki couldn't help but feel slightly scared at what she was about to do. Yes, she had been to the smallest island on the planet before, and she had come to no harm on her journey. However, this time was different. She had never gone hunting there before. She had never journeyed beyond the safety of her island to seek whatever creature it was that threatened her nation. For this reason, she was fearful. She looked down at her Prince, and slowly bowed her head. She had him by her side, and she had to keep him safe. She had powers beyond even her own understanding, and she swore to herself that she would use them to ensure both his and her safety on this trip.

One of the ship's crew-women pulled the anchor, and with it, the crowd gave a final cheer. The ship started forward instantly. Prince Hikaru nodded to his Queen as he stood at the helm, then turned to look deep into the distance. He saw nothing but water. The rich, blue colour seemed endless. It would be a long journey. No one knew when they would return.

Queen Fubuki took to the sky, flapping her blazing wings. Small whirlwinds of fire span off her as she flew higher. She didn't look back as she flew. She was too focused. Her nation needed her. She had to be their pillar of strength. It wouldn't take her a long time to fly to the small island. Prince Hikaru would take longer, but he would come eventually. She could already see a tiny dot in the distance. It was surrounded by so much sea that it could be easily mistaken for a whale simply drawing in breath. Closer and closer she flew. The dot became more visible. She flew as fast as she could, until the dot was no longer a dot, but the Volcano Island itself. She must have already flown half the distance. Prince Hikaru would still be in sight of the docks. Yet she continued on.

The island grew bigger and bigger. She was nearly there. She chanced a look behind her and saw only a vast, blue sea. How fast must she have flown? It was as though the island wanted to be found. Queen Fubuki knew all too well how the world she ruled was not held together by the physical laws of most planets. Hers was unruly. Hers was different. Macha Land was sometimes known to change shape, mainly in length. The Main Stage changed the most. Queen Fubuki created it that way. It was as alive as she was. The crystal floor would form magnificent pathways, platforms would float effortlessly around her, and the stage would even turn liquid beneath her. Her Songshows were truly a magickal spectacle to behold.

Queen Fubuki didn't know to what extent the smallest island of Macha Land could change its shape and mass. Maybe it couldn't at all. She had never stayed long enough to see for herself; nor had any living creature from the Main Island that she knew about. However, before long she would see just how mysterious this little island could be.

* * *

Prince Hikaru stood at the helm of the ship, when one of the crew-men brought Kaze up to see his Prince. The horse was like no other, and could not be kept down below deck. Hikaru stroked his mane again as the ship moved gently through the water.

The crew were hard at work, and the Four Guardians were resting together around a table. They had ale to drink and fruit to snack on. Prince Hikaru, however, remained at the helm. He didn't want to lose his focus. After losing sight of Queen Fubuki mere moments after setting sail, he didn't want to take his eyes away from the direction of their destination. He wanted to know that she was safe. If he saw even the slightest element of danger in the distance he would do whatever he could to help her. Yet as those thoughts of devotion went through Hikaru's mind, he realised that there was very little he could in fact do if anything were to happen to her. She was already miles ahead of them. He tricked himself into believing that he could already make out the island, but he knew deep down that it would be days before that would happen.

After hours of sailing, his face had become numb from the harsh sea air. Reluctantly, he gave up the helm to a trusted crew member and he finally took his eyes off the distant nothingness and looked around the ship. Kaze continued to move his head to the rhythm of the waves and paid Hikaru very little attention. The Bridge Over the River now seemed a lot smaller, and

Prince Hikaru could see the Main Island more clearly. Soon, Winter would be over and Queen Fubuki would withdraw the Veil of Warmth. Spring would bring its own mild warmth, and nature would blossom along with it. Prince Hikaru couldn't wait for Spring. He loved to spend his days sitting under the cherry blossom trees near the Palace and drinking fine wines all day with the Queen.

Hikaru's daydream was interrupted by a member of the crew calling out and pointing at something overboard. For a moment, Hikaru feared that someone had fallen out to sea. Unfortunately, he was wrong. Before Prince Hikaru could even react, the shadow underneath their ship had grown so large that he could see nothing else. The ship began to rise unnaturally. Seawater still reached over board and swarmed the deck. Crew members ran to their stations. Kaze leaped fearfully into the air and crashed through the wooden floor, falling painfully onto the lower deck. The Four Guardians were up and in formation immediately. Prince Hikaru just watched. He needed to see what it was.

The ship jolted to the right as the beast broke through the sea to their left. Water filled the air. Dark blue scales burst out from the ocean.

"Attack!" The Guardian named Strength called out to his brothers. Defence raised his shield high up in front of all of them. It was made of titanium and was too big for any of the other Guardians to even lift. Endurance pulled his bow and arrow and frantically started shooting his silver arrows at the weakest parts of the beast that he could see. Agility stood watching, waiting for his chance to jump from the ship onto the beast and attack with his daggers. But these four warriors were no match for a thing of this size. The beast was so large that what had nearly capsized their ship was but its left fin. It was easily big enough to swallow their ship in one fatal gulp.

Prince Hikaru stood frozen as the gigantic sea monster finally revealed its head. Fangs as large as the Palace's doors glistened in the light, and eyes as dark as night glared at the ship. There was no way they could fight this sea monster and hope to survive. It would consume them whole. In what he thought would be his last moments, Hikaru looked towards where Queen Fubuki would be - towards the Volcano Island. He prayed that she wouldn't come to the same fate.

A crash of wood brought him back, and splintered timber flew through the air. Crew members were clutching whatever part of the ship they could find, but some fell into the cold, deadly sea. Kaze panicked below deck. The Four Guardians kept trying to fight the beast, but only distracted it temporarily. Prince Hikaru knew that wouldn't last for much longer.

In a moment of heroism, Prince Hikaru drew his sword. Another present from the Queen, this sword was a simple bastard sword, with his name engraved into the handle. Hikaru ran to the bow of the ship, and leaped onto the beast. But he could barely reach it, and only managed to land on its lower back as it began to dive back into the water. The beast was building up momentum to attack again, but now Hikaru had stuck his sword deep into it and would be riding into the water too. He held on as tightly as he could as he plunged into the water. Without a moment's hesitation, Agility jumped onto the beast as well, just before it was completely submerged.

Agility managed to cut deep into what looked like the great monster's scaly tail. It sounded like metal slicing stone. He managed to pierce it. The creature roared with its head deep under water, with Hikaru still clutching on not far ahead. Bubbles of air reached the surface, echoing the screams of the monster. The half-beaten ship barely remained afloat. The battle raged onwards beneath it. Hikaru could not breathe and yet, with his eyes closed, he continued to hold on as the creature sank further and further down.

As he descended, Prince Hikaru realised that if the beast was breathing air like him. It would have to draw breath again soon. It was only a matter of time. But could he last as long as this gargantuan creature could? Darkness surrounded him as the creature refrained from another attack and instead swam further downwards. The cold icy waters could possibly kill Hikaru before the lack of air would. He was surely lost. His mind went blank and his grip began to loosen.

* * *

This island was naturally warmer than the largest of the three islands, due to the geothermal energy from the volcano itself. As the Phoenix, she welcomed the heat. There was no snow to be seen either, but the winds that blew through the island were chilling. From a distance, the island looked perfectly peaceful. Only a few birds could be seen circling above the trees. The volcano was calm and resting. She had finally made it here. The Volcano Island.

Queen Fubuki cascaded from the sky and swooped down along the waves as she closed in on the island. The ocean reached into a section of the landscape that looked like a small beach. Upon arriving at the beach, Queen Fubuki closed her Phoenix eyes, and the flames on her wings went out. The feathers started to fall off. Then, in a spectacular flash of fire, she burned away her Phoenix flesh, and out stepped Queen Fubuki in her human form. The feathers turned to golden ash, and danced along the sandy beach as the sea breeze scattered it away.

She stood there, skyclad, and watched the island with utter curiosity. It was quiet. Very quiet. The beach stretched no further than a quarter of a mile. To her left, she could see a small woods. Directly in front of her was the volcano. It was fairly large, but she could climb it by nightfall if she wanted to. To her right, there was what looked like a small wooden cabin. It was crafted by a living creature, but clearly not by one that had lived in this century. It was almost completely covered in moss and grass, and ivy had spread over the windows. It was so close to the beach that she decided to explore it last, as she could wait for Hikaru and the others to arrive while she did.

As she couldn't very well explore the island naked, Queen Fubuki conjured a humble outfit, which would be comfortable for her to explore in. She summoned her magickal staff and, in a blaze of fire, it appeared before her. With it held tightly in her right hand, she twisted and twirled on the beach, and the waves came and went beside her as she danced. From the top of her staff an amber-coloured liquid began to pour down onto her body. It stuck to her like honey, and enveloped her otherwise naked body. Eventually, the liquid began to set, and turn opaque. She lowered her staff, and chanted under her breath to finish the spell.

"Liquid amber trickling down, I conjure myself a golden gown." In a flash of pink light that shot from her left hand, the liquid turned into a golden fabric that was fitted perfectly to her body. It was a sleeveless half-gown that stopped at her waist.

For her bottoms, she walked over to the nearest tree, and picked three of the largest leaves she could find. She then sat facing the tree, crossed legged. With her back to the ocean, she began to pull the leaves apart, only to entwine them back together. Eventually she had enough fabric to mould herself a pair of shorts. She slid them on and chanted yet another rhyme to finish her spell. "These three leaves entwined together, will make the most protective leather".

She then picked up a fallen twig to form a belt, and crafted a pair of leather shoes from the bark of a different tree. "This here twig around my waist, ensure that all is held in place. Leather shoes from the bark of this tree, cast your protection unto me." Finally, she scooped up a large handful of sand, stood up, and started to sprinkle it in a circular motion in front of her.

"Sands of time, golden and warm,
I summon up a mighty storm,
Melt together and form my cape,
Do not let my heat escape.
Surround me in your love and light,
Protect me from the dark of night,
With this my outfit is now complete,
And the unknown evil I shall defeat!"

She chanted, this time fairly loudly, and the sand took shape into a soft, velvety cloak. The yellow sand turned a rich golden colour. This cloak would help shield her from the cruel, cold winds.

Queen Fubuki could of course have conjured any outfit that she desired, but instead she chose to make it from parts of the island. She would attract less attention from creatures on the island because her clothes were made from the same life energy as them. This outfit would also make another wonderful talisman. It would remind her of the journey she took to the Volcano Island, and of whatever evil she would face. Fubuki loved to create things, and often gave weapons and armour to her Prince, as a token of her undying love for him. She thought about giving him the golden cloak when he arrived at the island.

Now it was time to explore. She stood tall and strong, with her staff in hand. Her golden outfit glistened as she stared across the small island.

"Whoever you are, whatever you are... I am coming for you." She called out. A part of her knew she had been heard.

The woods to her left, which she now stood in front of, had an opening with a naturally formed path leading further into it. She could see already from where she was standing that it was only a short path that led to an opening deeper in the woods. Her search would start there. She took one last glance out at the sea, silently wished Hikaru a safe journey, and then began along the path. Trees either side of her had grown overhead, as if to form a tunnel. Bushes and smaller trees grew either side, but seemed to stop at the edge of this path. Underfoot, there was only gravel, twigs and leaves. Still, it was a pleasant enough path to walk along. The gorgeous greenery made her feel safe and connected to her planet.

Before long she had reached the opening, and as she looked behind her she could still see the small beach in the distance. She could still hear the waves crashing against the sand. Here in the opening of the woods, the trees had stopped growing, and instead there was a large clearing. It was almost perfectly circular, and inside this opening there was a small pond to her right. The ground was mostly flat here, but at the edge of the pond closest to her the ground seemed to be higher than anywhere else. She walked over to it, fascinated. It was nice to be free to explore as she pleased. Curiosity got the better of her, and she decided to lie down so that her head was hanging over the edge of the small hill. She could see herself in the water as she lay on her chest.

Her face stared back at her. She smiled at her own reflection. What an amusing island. As her long black hair escaped from behind her ears and hit the pond, the reflection blurred beneath her. The tips of her hair were wet. Water rippled outwards. Queen Fubuki looked up, and to her surprise she saw a small lion cub at the other end of the pond. It was so close that she could hear it slurping up the water. The lion cub paid no attention to her at all and instead was merrily filling its belly with fresh water. What was a lion cub doing here on this island? Was there an entire pride out here?

Queen Fubuki continued to think to herself about what she was seeing, until a sudden rumble from the volcano caused her to jolt with terror, and the lion cub to scamper away back into the forest.

"What was that?" Fubuki called out to herself. Suddenly she wished Hikaru were here with her. Fear was slowly taking over her. She got to her feet, not taking her eyes off the volcano. It was large enough for her to see it above the trees. Then, at the very top, she noticed it again. The black figure from before. Except this time, it was a lot closer and a lot clearer.

He looked down at her in disgust. Then with another rumble and a flash of black lightning, he disappeared from above the volcano, only to reappear behind her. Queen Fubuki quickly span around, and pointed her staff out threateningly in front of her. The black figure was a young man, with dirty blonde hair. He was tall and slim. He had a somewhat childish face, but with eyes that looked wise beyond his years. His soul was tainted, and a darkness filled him that she had never known before.

"I am the King of Truth," he proclaimed. His voice was deep and sorrowful. "I have come for you."

"You... You were the one who attacked my people! You were the one who killed that innocent!" Queen Fubuki felt enraged. How dare he introduce himself. Soon he would pay for what he had done and this would all be over. She would avenge the poor man who had died.

"He will not be the last, I guarantee you. Your realm is mine. You will die too!" His words were sharp and cold. Fubuki had barely any time to react. The terrifying man raised his hands into the air, and a bolt of black lightning struck down from above.

The sky started to turn grey and the air was thick. Queen Fubuki flicked her staff upwards, and swung it forcefully in the King of Truth's direction. A huge gust of wind picked up from behind her and threw him into the air. His black robes twisted around him. Even as he resisted, he hit the top of a tree and landed on the ground. He grunted. But he quickly got to his feet.

"Why are you doing this? Who are you?" Fubuki screamed at him.

"You know why. You know exactly who I am." He spoke to her as if they had known each other for years, and yet she had never seen him before in her life.

"Hikari no chikara!" Fubuki called out into the sky. White orbs of light grew from nothing, and suddenly exploded into violent whirlwinds of dust. The King of Truth shielded his eyes and, with his right hand outstretched in front of him, spat out an enormous fireball. With both hands, he threw the fireball into the air and it absorbed the energy from the dusty whirlwinds. Before it could consume Fubuki, she turned into her Phoenix form. The fire hit her, but it only made her stronger.

In another burst of flames, she turned back into her human form to fight. She danced past shots of black lightning, attempting to retrieve the staff that she had dropped. The King of Truth, seeing this, extended his left hand, and it flew to him within seconds. The golden staff turned a dark purple colour as his hand touched the handle.

The King of Truth cackled with what energy he had left. Gaining control of the Queen's staff had drained him heavily. All Queen Fubuki could do was look on in shock. She felt her heart ache. He must have been connected to her in some way to be able to take her staff like that. The staff was a part of her. She was devastated. The King of Truth held the staff high in the air, drawing upon her power. Before she could make her next move, a bolt of black lightning larger than he had ever conjured hit her right in the stomach. She fell to the floor, and cried out in pain. He was just as weak as her, and knew he didn't have enough strength to defeat her here.

"This is not over. I will have my Kingdom back." The King of Truth declared. He had much bigger plans. As a final bolt of black lightning enveloped him he disappeared into the sky.

Hikaru... My love. I need you. Come to me...

* * *

Water burst from his mouth as Prince Hikaru gained consciousness. He was alive. His body was still numb from the cold, and he was so weak that he could not even lift his head to see where he was. He couldn't hear anything through the pain. He just looked up at the sky and let his eyes adjust to the light.

"Do you think it will come back and attack us again?" Defence asked. Defence was a huge man, with muscles that were twice the size of Hikaru's. His shield was flat on the floor, and he sat on a stool, his arm resting on his knee, thinking. His other hand held a goblet filled with ale.

"I cannot say. Let us hope it does not." Agility's voice was still fragile. He had been under for as long as Prince Hikaru, but he was more resilient. Agility was lean but muscular, and his legs were his strongest feature. He could outrun anyone at full speed.

Endurance and Strength were both light skinned and had blonde and brown hair. They were sitting by Prince Hikaru's side, keeping him warm and alive. They were always together. They had their handfasting ceremony not three moons ago, which the Queen herself had attended. They wore the same deep red, leather armour. As they took care of him, Hikaru began to adjust to the pain and could almost move his limbs again.

"At least our ship is still afloat. Our Queen will be able to spell it back to shape when we get to the Volcano Island." Strength said. His voice was soft and pleasing.

"*If* we get there. The main sail is gone. The ship's structure is falling apart. We could sink before we arrive at the island," Defence argued, swigging his ale as he spoke.

"But we are moving, slowly but surely. We will get there eventually. The Goddess is on our side, we must not fear." Endurance's smile was enchanting. He was always the optimist. Hikaru began to move next to him. He moaned in agony.

"What happened?" Hikaru muttered, before raising his head and letting out a groan. Endurance slid a feather-filled cushion beneath his head that he had fetched from the sleeping quarters below deck. "Is Kaze...?"

"Your mount is fine. Although still very frightened. He won't let anyone close to him." Agility started to explain how he had saved the Prince. "You eventually lost your grip on the beast, along with your consciousness. I noticed this and somehow managed to hold on until I got to you. I swam us back to the surface as fast as I could." The dark-skinned warrior grinned with pride. And rightfully so. He knew how pleased the Queen would be after hearing his tale of bravery.

"My friend. I owe you my life." Hikaru raised a hand to him, thanking him with all the strength he could muster. "The beast, will it return? Are we safe?" The four warriors smiled at each other as they had only just discussed this amongst themselves.

"Worry not. We are on course for the Volcano Island. The Queen will be waiting for us. She may even be ready to leave by the time we arrive." Strength was trying to reassure his Prince that the danger had passed.

"My Queen... I cannot wait to lay eyes on her once more. I thought I..." Hikaru closed his eyes and paused. "I thought I never would again."

It took three times as long as planned, but eventually the ship made it to the Volcano Island. It was agreed that since the ship was in great need of repair, the crew and the Four Guardians would stay behind to work on it.

The crew brought the ship to shore, and began repairing it straight away. Endurance and Strength started working on a fire, whilst Defence found a good spot to sit and drink his ale. Agility, still not fully recovered, stood on the beach and simply looked out to sea. That beast was still out there, and would want its revenge.

Queen Fubuki would already have had days to explore the tiny island, so having appeased the frightened Kaze, Hikaru set off in search of his Queen. From the ship, the island had looked so small that Hikaru was confident it wouldn't take him more than a day to find her.

Prince Hikaru waved farewell to the party and trotted along towards the centre of the island. He saw the volcano, and the small wooden cabin far off to the right, and the forest to his left. He couldn't wait to see her, to see his beloved. So much had happened to him, and he couldn't wait to tell her everything. She would surely be missing him too by now. He decided to ride West through the woods, and then circle back along the edge of the Volcano and back to the beach.

He could see what he assumed to be the Queen's footsteps in the sand, as the small beach gave way to the grass from the woods. Kaze was still so irritable. He kept trying to turn back towards the ship, but Hikaru forced him onwards. Tired from struggling with the black mount, he decided to veer off the main path through the woods, and trotted left, past the line of trees.

While keeping the path in sight, Prince Hikaru continued to trot through the woods at a leisurely pace. The weather was cold, but warmer than the depths of the ocean. The sun was still high in the sky, and Hikaru thought he could even hear birds singing in the distance. What type of birds would live on such a fascinating island? He couldn't wait to see.

His mind started to focus on the Queen. Where was she? Was she safe? He assumed that she didn't see the large sea creature that had attacked them, otherwise she would have come to help fight it. She had to be somewhere on the island. Hikaru started to worry for her. Had she found what it was that had poisoned the poor villager that night at her Songshow? If so, would she have tried to stop whatever it was on her own? Hikaru hoped that she would have more sense than that, and would have waited for him. Perhaps she was worried for Hikaru as well. They were days later than scheduled. Perhaps she was alone somewhere waiting for their arrival. He couldn't know. All Hikaru could do was look for her now. The island looked peaceful enough. Surely he was worrying over nothing. She must be safe ashore. He imagined her blissfully meditating at the summit of the volcano, looking down on him at this very moment.

As he looked behind him to check on the party, Prince Hikaru was hit with a striking sense of confusion. Had he taken a wrong turn? The beach was no longer behind him as it had been only seconds ago, but instead woods stretched as far as his eyes could see. It was the same ahead of him. To his right. To his left. Just woods. The path he had been following was also gone.

"How can this be?" He questioned aloud. "Fubuki!" He called in panic. "My Queen!" The miles and miles of trees and foliage that seemed to have appeared around him swallowed his words whole. Yet again, he was enclosed within nothing but nature. How could he have been so foolish as to leave on a search on his own? He kicked Kaze into a gallop and rode as fast as his remaining strength would allow in the direction he was originally going. If it were a trick of the forest, he would have to outdo it with willpower alone.

He kept riding. Trees and bushes became a blurry mess as he rushed past them. The cold air hit his face and brought tears to his eyes. Kaze rode bravely beneath him, sensing that something was wrong. It became apparent to him that if the island could trick him with such ease that perhaps his Queen was in danger too. He had to find her, he had to save her.

However, it was no use. The further he rode into the endless stretch of trees, the more the island engulfed him. Lost in the wilderness and giving up his attempt to run through the endless forest, Hikaru brought Kaze to a halt.

"What should I do?" He asked both the horse and himself. "How do we get out of here?" Panic and desperation made his voice quiver. The trees were so tall around him that he couldn't even tell where the volcano was anymore. They reached up as high as he could see. What little light managed to break through the treetops was all Hikaru had. Kaze collapsed to the forest floor from exhaustion. Hikaru looked down at his mount. "I guess you're right, all we can do is wait here. Maybe she'll find us..."

* * *

It felt like she had been calling him for a lifetime. Surely soon he would find her.

My love. I need you. Hikaru, please.

She hadn't moved from the spot where the King of Truth had struck her down. Her body was paralysed. Queen Fubuki had been defeated. She couldn't believe it. This was the evil that she knew was coming for her all along. How was she going to defeat someone so full of hatred?

Fubuki didn't have enough ethereal energy to cast any more spells. She could barely even move. Instead, all she could do was lie there and wait for her Prince. She felt like he was a world away from her, when in truth they were so close. It would nonetheless be a very long time before he would find her. The Volcano Island had claimed him. He was lost in the woods now.

The King of Truth had taken her staff from her. She couldn't let that happen. With the last burst of energy she had left, she envisioned the staff before her. Black lightning appeared above her and she saw it not an arm's reach away. It was trapped in a purple void. Painfully, she reached her hand in and grabbed it. A sharp stinging pain shot up her arm. With a final pull, she took it back and the black lightning vanished with a bang. Slowly the staff lost its purple glow and went back to the golden shimmering colour it always was.

She closed her eyes, and clenched her stomach. Her arm was in agony. Her golden clothes had turned black with soot and ash. The pain was so intense that she felt herself losing her life energies, and began slipping away into a deep, deep darkness. The cold Winter's night fell on her, as she lay there alone in the small opening of the forest. Birds stopped singing their birdsong, and a haunting silence fell upon the world of Macha Land.

Before I knew it, six months had passed since I had started working at the Italian restaurant. Everyone was lovely, and I had settled in to my new life well. I was still living with Georgina, but we had swapped rooms to offset my lower income. Georgina was over the moon to get the extra space.

I was on the same bus I took every day, from Camden all the way to Tottenham Court Road. The shift pattern that I now worked meant that, while the journeys were a lot quieter, they felt a lot more dangerous since I was coming home so late at night. Yet, even though I did get funny looks from time to time, I rarely had to deal with anything worse than that. Rarely.

It was winter in London now. People's breath shimmered in the dark of night. Shivering smokers huddled outside glowing pubs. I had bought a large, navy blue coat with red buttons and a furry hood. It wasn't quite enough to keep me warm, so I also wore a long red scarf that came down to my knees. I always snuggled into it after a long day at work, with my headphones in, as I made my journeys home. Sometimes I would wrap it around me twice and cover half my face.

Georgina's birthday was coming up. She had really been there for me this year, so I wanted to do something special. Before my shift started I decided to walk around the shops along Tottenham Court Road to see if I could find her a decent present. She was into the colour black at the moment, so I was looking for black clothes, and maybe a nice set of black candles, or a little black book. I loved buying presents and wrapping them up. I was even thinking of making Georgina a small gothic style hamper.

One of my closest friends from the restaurant was walking towards me when she spotted me.

"Beam! How ya' doin'?" Alysha was always buzzing. She rarely came in without an energy drink in her hand. "Lookin' good as always!" She smiled.

"Hey Alysha, you working the late shift too?" I was glad. Working at the restaurant was always more fun with her. Sometimes, when the boss wasn't in, she would bring "work juice" up to the second floor and we would sip it together where the cameras couldn't see.

"Yeah! You headin' there now?"

"Sure, can do. I was just window shopping."

We walked along together in the direction of the restaurant. I was still looking in shop windows and Alysha was smoking. Her hair was braided, so she tied it up when she started work. She was already wearing her black uniform, with a baggy hoody over the top that I assumed belonged to her boyfriend. Her nails were painted beautiful, bright colours, but cut short. The owner of the restaurant was always complaining about her style, but she paid him no notice. I admired that.

My hair had grown out of the pixie cut, but was still fairly short. It wasn't long enough to style with straighteners, but I at least now had a fringe that I could play with. On nights when I would stand at the door to welcome customers in and organise the bookings, I didn't have to serve any food. That meant that I could wear my own clothes, and experiment more with my hair. I always loved those shifts so much more.

"Beam, we are still so early! Fancy a cheeky cocktail before we start?" Alysha grinned and pulled my arm before I could say no. There was a stylish bar close enough to the restaurant to get there in minutes but far enough away to not risk being seen by anyone else. Like giggling school girls we ran into the bar and went to our usual table around the corner. The waiter nodded to us and started preparing our drinks without us even having to say a word. He was used to seeing us around this time of day, as we finished around now when we worked the lunch shift.

The waiter brought over a Sex on the Beach for Alysha, and a Mojito for me. He clearly fancied Alysha, as he always tried to make small talk with her, despite her monosyllabic answers. Alysha was so strong and independent. I aspired to be like her so much. She had such a fun and exciting life. I sipped my cocktail and relaxed into my chair.

"I'm so tired..." Alysha said suddenly.

"Why's that? We haven't even started working yet," I replied.

"Literally *no* sleep last night..." Alysha looked up from her drink and burst out laughing. "Lately he's been relentless!" She said through the laughter.

"Stop complaining girl, I'm jealous!"

"Well go out and get some, B. You're single, right?" Alysha hit me on the right shoulder with one hand, and she sipped her drink with her left. I laughed even louder in shock.

"As if! I think I'm miles away from that happening. Seriously... no one is into me at the moment."

"Shut up, you are beautiful. Don't let anyone tell you differently." The conversation suddenly turned serious, so I hid behind my drink.

"I have far too much going on in my head at the moment." I smiled, but it was a sad smile.

"Like what babes?"

"Alysha, I've known you for a while now... can I tell you something crazy?"

"Anything. Spill. You're dating eight guys at once, aren't you? Knew it!" We laughed again. She was always so full of joy, I loved being around her.

"Be serious for a minute!" I giggled again. "OK, so seriously. I'm going to tell you. I..." I made sure to lower my voice. "About half a year ago, I went to hospital. A mental health hospital to be exact. Because of... everything. Basically, I think I'm insane. Almost every night I have these crazy dreams. And like, in the dreams I am this amazing Queen, with all kinds of magical powers. I'm like, the ruler of this whole island thing. And I have a husband, and we go on journeys together, and do all kinds of spells and stuff." For the first time since leaving the hospital, I told someone about the lengths that my mind had gone to constructing this parallel world. I told her all about the fictional characters, the places, the stories, and she listened carefully to every word.

"I've smoked some shit in my time, but wow... you are on a whole other level B." She sounded half amazed and half shocked. I was trying to analyse her reaction. Our glasses were both empty as we sat there together. "I gotta' say, I know you have gone through some shit, clearly, but this fictional Queen character, I mean it does all make sense, right?"

"I guess it does. I feel like she is who I'm meant to be sometimes, ya' know?" It felt so good to finally tell someone, and have them listen.

"Are you trying to tell me that you got magic powers B? You gonna' try and make my glass float or some shit?" Alysha joked.

"No, don't be stupid!" I laughed along with her. She was so lovely. I really felt like I could trust her.

"Well, I don't know what to say Beam. You have an amazing imagination. You should write a book or something. God knows you've been through enough in your life."

"Maybe you're right. I'm... happy though. Me, now. After everything, I'm truly happy."

"Well good babes, you deserve to be happy. I hope you go on to be even happier as things continue to change."

"Alysha, that's really sweet of you. Thank you." We were so deep in conversation that I had forgotten about work. My eyes drifted to the clock behind the bar, and I bolted upright as I realised.

"Shit! Alysha, it's gone six, we should go!" I grabbed my bag and scarf.

"Oh right, yeah! So, you all good B?" Alysha checked before we ran out the door. Her hand rested on my shoulder.

"I'm good, thanks. Just don't tell anyone I was in a mental ward, ok?" I smiled.

"Of course. Just don't be acting like a crazy Queen at work, ok Queen B?" She laughed and put her winter coat on.

"Promise!"

* * *

The evening went quickly, mainly because I started my shift slightly drunk. The Mojito had gone straight to my head. That meant that we were smiling and giggling the entire shift. Paul, the manager, was happy as the customers gave us great feedback. He was a sweet guy who had been working at the restaurant for a couple of years.

"Maybe we should have a cocktail before work every day, ay' B!" Alysha whispered when the manager left us to get ready to go home. The restaurant had only a couple of tables left, and they were already on their desserts. Alysha and I were late to start, but as we were the only ones who were working the lunch shift the next day, we were allowed to go early.

I would usually go to the staff toilet and take off all my makeup before heading home. It felt safer that way. I felt like I drew less attention to myself. But I was so tired that I decided to just go straight home. There was hardly anyone around this late at night anyway.

It was 11 p.m. when we left. It was dark. It was only a Tuesday, so the streets were empty. Alysha went home on the tube, and left me at the bus stop, after hugging me goodbye. It felt so good to have told her about my weird dreams. It was different to when I told the doctors on the ward. She wasn't analysing me, she was just listening.

"Get home safe!" I called out. She waved at me and turned to run for the tube. Her boyfriend was no doubt waiting for her at home.

I was tired and cold, but I enjoyed my job so much, so it was worth it. It made my office job seem so boring and slow paced. It felt like everything had happened exactly how it should have. As if it was fate.

"Hey sweetie, what you doin' here all by yourself?" A stranger's voice filled the cold air. Shit.

"Erm... just on my way home. Thanks." I tried to be dismissive, but not rude enough to provoke anger. I was petrified. What did he want? I wished he would just go away.

"Want some company?" He moved closer. His aftershave was horrible. He was tall, pale, wore a black suit and had his hair cut short. Cleanly shaven. He was an attractive guy. He didn't look like someone who would be desperate enough to hit on a random person at a bus stop. He was looking around, almost nervously. Was he checking we were alone?

"No, I'm honestly fine." I tried to be more firm. Should I run away? The restaurant was only around the corner. Paul would be there, he would keep me safe. He was so understanding. But could I even outrun this guy?

"What? Why so shy?" He sat next to me at the bus stop. He wasn't touching me, but he was staring at me intensely. There was no one else around, only me and this stranger. I couldn't decide if I should run for it, or if I should try and talk my way out of trouble. Where was this fucking bus?

"Look, I'm flattered, but I'm not interested. Please just leave me alone." The words tumbled out of my mouth. I wished I was the Queen from my dreams.

"I can be a gentleman. I won't hurt you. Someone like you shouldn't be so picky." His words cut like knives. How fucking rude! My fear turned into a rush of anger that coursed through my body. How dare he? I looked around. No one. Maybe I could hit him and run. I was fairly strong, after all. "Oh, I'm sorry… That sounded really rude. I didn't mean it like that. I meant it in that you are… special. Right? Don't worry, I've always wanted to be with a special kind of girl like you…" He grinned and slowly placed his hand on my upper thigh. I felt instantly sick. I jumped up and elbowed him in the jaw without even really meaning to. He called out in pain and grabbed my arm, and I heard what sounded like his suit jacket ripping. "You fucking bitch, come here!" he screamed. His voice was angry and frustrated. He was stronger than he looked and he pulled me back to him.

"Fuck off!" I wriggled and tried to break free. His cold hands were on me, freezing me like ice. Touching me. Shattering me.

"Shut the fuck up." His left hand reached up and tried to cover my mouth. "Stop resisting. You know you want it." I bit him. He screamed again. I turned around and kneed him in his groin. I freed myself from his grasp and ran so fast that my bag was spilling out all over the road. I could hear my things hitting the ground, but I didn't care. I didn't stop. I just had to keep running. The dark sky made it hard to find my way, but I managed to follow the empty street back to the restaurant. I hadn't noticed I was crying. But tears streamed down my cheeks. I was shivering. I wiped the tears away, only to let more take their place.

When I got back to the restaurant Paul was sitting there cashing up at table seven. The owner had gone home. I banged on the door. I didn't realise how frightened I was, and noticed that my hands were also shaking. Tears were still running down my cold, red face. Paul looked up, and ran over straight away. He looked so concerned, I almost felt bad involving him.

"Beam? What the hell happened? Are you ok?" He opened the door and pulled me in. After locking the door back up, he pulled out a chair for me to sit on. "Did someone attack you?"

"I'm sorry to come back here. No, well... I guess not. Not really. Some guy just tried to... he was..." My voice trailed off and tears started flowing again. My makeup must have looked terrible, I should have taken it off. Maybe this would have never happened. I sank down further into my chair. Paul slammed his hand on the table.

"That fucking bastard! Which way did he go?"

"No Paul, don't do anything. It's fine. I ran away before he could do anything serious. I'm fine, I'm just shaken up."

"I'll call the police. Go and help yourself to a drink, you poor thing." Paul nodded towards the bar area while he grabbed his phone from his bag.

"No! Paul, please. No. It's too embarrassing, you can't!" I put my hand over his to stop him. The only thing worse than that experience would be having to explain it to a room full of policemen. I just couldn't, it was too embarrassing.

"But B..." Paul's face dropped. He looked so worried.

"Paul, it's fine. I just want to stay here for a while. Nothing happened. I ran away before it could."

"Ok. I guess it's your decision, but then that bastard is out there..." Paul looked through the glass of the restaurant door. His long, brown hair was tied back in a short ponytail, and yet he still looked very masculine. "I'll get you a drink, fancy some wine? I could use a glass myself."

Paul grabbed a bottle of red and we drank it together. When he could see that I had calmed down and my tears had dried he ordered us a cab each. Paul paid for both. He clearly hadn't planned to stay this late either. Outside it was starting to get light, and a warm red haze was filling up the streets of London. I had to be back at work soon, so all I wanted to do was climb into bed and wrap myself in my pink duvet.

In my head, all I could hear were that bastard's words. *A special kind of girl like you.* I had been so close to getting seriously hurt. This was all too much. All I was to him was a fantasy. A fetish. My only purpose was to fulfil his... curiosities. Just a toy to play with. Something less than human. My heart ached. That was my biggest fear. What if that was my only purpose? All I would ever be was... *a special kind of girl.*

The sky was dark purple. An occasional flash of lightning was the only light. Rain fell from the clouds above and hit the floor around her as she lay in the same spot. She was still and lifeless, like an old doll stuck on a shelf. All her body could do was try to gather strength. She had still not woken from the slumber that the King of Truth had left her in. He had defeated her, but she wouldn't let that happen again.

With Queen Fubuki in a deep black void between life and death, the rest of the creatures of Macha Land had been frozen in time too, however the seasons had not. The creatures of Macha Land were in a slumber, just as their Queen was. Summer had taken the land. The white snows had melted away and the cold winds had calmed. The Ice Mountain had melted down into the Lake. It was a vast lake, spreading miles and miles to the furthest Eastern regions of Macha Land. It was deep and would usually have been filled with mermaids and mermen who would have returned from the South, had they not been frozen in time. The South was now no longer a beach, but the Southern Desert, and this year the desert was far larger than it had ever been. The Veil of Warmth, that usually defended against the harshness of Winter, now brought a new-found suffering in Summer.

Prince Hikaru spent a long time searching for Fubuki in the woods of the Volcano Island before time stopped. He had continued to look for his Queen, whilst hunting for food and making fires wherever possible. His Queen's horse Kaze followed him closely and drank from pools of water in the woods. When Queen Fubuki fell into her deep sleep, he was saved from the endless hunt that he was trapped in. The birds stopped singing. The trees stopped swaying in the wind. The waves calmed. All of Macha Land came to a standstill, and would remain that way until Queen Fubuki returned to bring life back to her world once again.

Within Queen Fubuki's mind was nothing but darkness. Black. Death. Until suddenly, a small, white orb of light came into the centre of her mind's eye. It grew larger until she could see into it. It was a view from above. She was looking down at herself. Looking down at everything. She could see the clouds beneath her, and from far, far above she could see the Main Island. The entirety of Macha Land in fact. All three islands. She was in the sky, looking down at her planet. It was made up of so much sea, so much blue. To the East, she could see the largest island. It looked small from up here. South West was the second island. It was just dust and sand. North of that would be the smallest island, where she was sleeping, but it was far too small to see from way up here.

She was an astral projection of herself. Flying around as light as air. While her body lay still on the Volcano Island, she was also looking down from high above the entire planet, watching everything. She floated, weightless. She was air itself. She was a Goddess. Or was she with the Goddess? Was the Goddess letting her see this in her dreams for a reason? What was happening? As her head filled with questions, she gently drifted down towards the planet. She was just above the clouds. She could just about make out the ocean beneath her, but around her it was thick, humid and moist. Fubuki didn't look like her normal self though. Her body was pale, almost transparent. She felt her body getting heavy and wet. The water from the clouds soaked her, and she felt herself fill up until she couldn't stay in the air any longer. The air rushed up around her, and she was falling towards the ocean.

She barely caught a glimpse of the Volcano Island in the distance as she crashed into the sea. Blue sprays of water splashed around her, as her body imbibed the ocean. She was no longer a wisp of air. Instead, she was connected to the entire sea, and enveloped the planet effortlessly. She hugged the earth beneath her like a mother holding her child. Gravity pulled her in, and kept her warm and calm.

Eventually, Fubuki managed to pull what felt like a body together, and it continued to get heavier. She sank further and further down into the depths of the sea. She felt emotional. Lonely. She wanted Hikaru back. The sunlight couldn't reach her anymore, as she hit the planet's crust. Miles and miles of sea were above her now, crushing her. It pushed her into the rocks and sand and stone.

Her astral body was between the weight of the ocean and the hardness of what was beneath it. She lost all sense of weight and gravity, until she was finally one with the rocks. The stones and sand were inside her, and she in them. No longer did she struggle against her heavy emotions, she was now stable. For what seemed like a lifetime, Fubuki remained within those rocks. Stones became metals. Metals became lava. She was within it, every centimetre. Every inch. Every particle. She was the planet. She was omnipresent.

However, she couldn't let herself stay there forever. She had to keep going, keep fighting. She let herself go deeper into the earth's core, until it was too warm for her to handle. She felt her body of stone fall apart. The heat encased her and she cracked under the pressure. Like Mercury prior to being frozen, she melted down. Her astral self fell away and turned to liquid lava. It burned her fears and terrors away. The fires of the world gave her strength and power. She could do anything. She was the Phoenix. She was almighty.

Magickal energy started to build within her, and she started to gain consciousness. Gradually, as it built, she could feel herself flowing upwards. As heat rises, so did she. The layers of the planet went by her, one by one, she felt the lava around her and within her rushing to the surface. It bubbled and boiled, until it shot out from the hard, warm rocks and burst out into the cooling skies. She flew outwards, spreading her Phoenix wings and stretching her claws.

"Quaa!" She roared as her wings opened up and the lava solidified on the earth beneath her. Her flames swirled around her as she stood on the edge of the volcano, looking around her once more. From up here, she could see everything a lot clearer. It was all frozen still, but she could see it. Fubuki looked down into the woods, and saw herself lying there. The snow had melted away and left her there, dirty and helpless. She saw Prince Hikaru, sleeping in the forest, with Kaze by his side and the small beach where the Four Guardians slumbered. The world of Macha Land was waiting for her to come back to them. Nothing was awake, no one was moving without her.

She glided down softly towards the small beach. The patterns on her wings danced orange and red as the air went through them like embers in a fire pit. Hey eyes were deep and black. She was a butterfly on fire. The lava had cooled and turned to dark black ash and rocks. The clouds above her were heavy and grey. If her world hadn't been so still, she could have mistaken it for a Summer storm.

In a burst of flames, she shed her Phoenix skin, and took her human form again. Her skin was still pale and transparent, and her hair flowed effortlessly down around her. She walked over to the small, wooden cabin on this small, mysterious island. Nature had grown wild and had taken it over. Fubuki grabbed the door and pulled it open with all her strength. It opened just enough for her to get inside.

Inside was dark, since all the windows were overgrown with bushes and trees. The only light around was coming in with her. She stepped forward with her back to the door. Her eyes adjusted to the light and she saw a small cauldron kept in a pit, deep in the middle of the room. It was surrounded by steps reaching up to each wall. Down was the only direction Fubuki could go.

She could see two chairs beyond the cauldron up by the farthest wall. They were empty, dusty and frail. She walked into the sunken floor and stared over the bottomless cauldron. The door shut behind her and blackness consumed her once again. Was she back in her mind's eye? Had she ever even left?

As she continued to gaze into the cauldron in front of her, she started to see shapes. She saw Hikaru, deep within the ocean, then lost in the woods. Then she saw him burning under the hot blazing sun and blown about by furious winds. Four trials of the elements. She saw a different man, one she recognised from years ago. A close friend who had known her soul, and loved her. She remembered his smile and it filled her with warmth. She saw him hugging her. Protecting her. But what about her Prince?

Deeper in the scrying pool of the cauldron Fubuki saw a young woman. Long, flowing, brown hair scattered with golden strands. She was very tall, and curvy. Feminine. She was smiling. Then she saw a little boy. He was a sad boy, confused and alone. He wanted to be different, he wanted to be himself. She saw the boy crying and howling like a wolf as he walked home alone.

Wake up. A voice echoed from outside the cabin. Fubuki shot upwards and ran to the door. My Queen, come back. It was Prince Hikaru, calling out to her amidst his own slumber. Fubuki kicked open the door, and hurried outside. The world was still untouched and silent, and yet she had heard him. It had to be him. She ran through the woods, and followed down the path she had come from in her physical body all that time ago. She could see the opening in the woods, and eventually got back to her body. For a brief moment she stood above herself, watching. She had grown stronger from this vision quest, but only in her mind. She would still need more time before she had her magickal energy back in full. Fubuki knew she would need it to defeat the King of Truth, so gathering it again was what she had to do. No matter how long it took her.

As she kneeled down by her physical body, her astral self felt drawn to it. It pulled her back in and eventually Queen Fubuki woke from her deep dark slumber. With a gasp of air, the four elements were with her and the world came back to life in an instant. The tides started to stir. Rain fell from the dark grey clouds. The birds started to sing and the trees moved in the wind. The Summer heat was on her skin. She felt tired and unclean. Getting to her feet she stretched out her body and dove into the small lake where the lion cub once drank from. The soot and dirt washed away from her in seconds. She was purified and cleansed.

"Trees that move and leaves that fall,
Birds that sing and bugs that crawl,
Reveal my Prince and let him be,
Bring my true love back to me.
For several moons you've kept him there,
Now end his pain and my despair,
Powers gained from an everlong dream,
Show me him, with this light beam!"

With that spell, a beam of light came down from the clouds and opened up a pathway from the woods. The leaves and branches coiled away and Prince Hikaru was there. He opened his eyes to see the wall of the woods had been broken away and he was closer to his Queen than either of them could have imagined. There were barely a hundred yards between them. Kaze woke startled and cantered towards his Queen. Hikaru threw his hands up against the blinding light. As soon as Hikaru saw his beloved Queen, he wasted no time in running towards her.

The beam of light stopped and Fubuki fell back to the side of the lake after she had climbed out. The spell had taken more energy from her than it should have.

She fell to her knees, weakened, yet happy to see his beautiful face once more. For months Fubuki had been trapped between life and death. It would be a long while until she had her powers back to normal, but it would be worth it. She would grow stronger than ever. For now she closed her eyes, feeling tired and weak.

Without words, they looked at each other. She fell into his embrace. Prince Hikaru lifted her gently onto Kaze and followed on after. They rode towards the small beach. It was over and they were back together. What she had seen had made her stronger. His warmth made her sleepy, so she closed her eyes. They were together again. For now, that was all that mattered.

A couple of days passed before I was ready to go back to work. I didn't go in the day after the assault, like I was meant to, as Paul had left me a message saying to take some time off. I spent most of those days in my pyjamas with Georgina freaking out at the end of my bed. When I was ready to go back outside, I walked to a coffee shop on my road and sat with a coffee for a couple of hours. I had lost all my confidence. I couldn't even go outside at first, but I knew I had to eventually. Georgina was with me, as it was the weekend. She brought me ice cream and we got pizza two days in a row.

"What a bastard. I mean, what the fuck. What an actual bastard." Georgina was still ranting as she bit into her pizza slice. Pineapple fell onto her plate. I was already finished with my pizza and had started on my ice cream.

"It's ok – he didn't actually do anything," I lied. He had touched me. It could have been a lot worse, I know, but I still felt so violated. That area... That area was the part of me I hated most.

Before long, I was back at work and things were mostly back to normal. Paul usually let me go home a bit earlier, except for Friday and Saturday nights when it was extremely busy. Sometimes we would get walk-ins as late as 10 p.m. When that happened, I had to stay quite late. That was ok, since the streets were a lot busier on weekends, so I didn't feel in as much danger. For my first week back, Alysha accompanied me to the bus stop where it happened and waited for me to be safely on the bus before running off to get the tube. Paul had also been treating me so kindly since that night. A part of me wanted to believe that he had started to fall for me. It felt like he really saw me as the person I wanted to be. But like I had said to Alysha, there was no way I was ready for that. I was surrounded by loving, caring people who did so much for me – that was all I needed for now.

One night, Alysha and I finished work early. It was only 10 p.m., and for some reason the restaurant was nearly empty. Paul said that there might be a rush of customers later on, but he would handle it. So we headed off.

London was bursting with Christmas decorations. Blue, yellow and red lights hung from building to building. Huge, green Christmas trees with beautifully wrapped, empty boxes beneath them, filled the shop windows all the way along Tottenham Court Road. Lights cascaded from glass towers, creating a golden glow in the snowy sky. It was cold outside and people rubbed their hands together to keep warm. On top of the lower buildings, I could see perfect, white blankets. Snow had settled and covered everything beneath it. Hustling shoppers with too many bags swarmed the streets like scattering mice. The snow on the ground turned from a powdery white dust into a grey sludge.

Alysha and I were different. We had time to spare and no intention of rushing. She asked me to come with her while she walked about the streets of London, looking for ideas for her boyfriend's Christmas present. I had already finished my Christmas shopping for my family, Georgina, Alysha and a few other close friends. I decided a card would be enough for the rest of the group from work.

"Why don't you get him a game or something?" I suggested as we walked past a game shop with second hand consoles and phones in the window. "Does he play anything?"

"Yeah, I think he was hinting for a PlayStation 4, 'cause all his mates have one. No chance though, I wasn't planning on spending that much on him." We chuckled and carried on walking. As we walked amongst the other shoppers who were finishing up, suddenly a face started smiling in my direction.

"Lizzy?" I screamed out as I realised who it was. "Oh my god, Lizzy!" She looked at me in amazement.

"Well look at you... Wow!" Her jaw almost hit the floor. I blushed. "How long has it been?"

"Like, years?"

"Bloody hell. You look amazing, but still you." Her mouth was still wide open. I smiled with embarrassment, and realised Alysha was standing next to me and had no idea who this was.

"Alysha, this is my friend from secondary school, Lizzy." I stood in between them. It always made me nervous when my old friends met my new friends.

"Hey, nice to meet you!" Lizzy smiled warmly.

"Yeah, you too!" Alysha did the same.

"I'm just about finished with my shopping and was on my way home, fancy a drink? Looks like you have lots to tell me about!" Lizzy grinned. She seemed genuinely happy for me. Alysha smiled too, as she could obviously tell what was going on.

We made our way to a quiet pub about five minutes off a side street. Everywhere else was far too busy to be able to chat properly to each other. Lizzy hadn't changed at all. She still had frizzy, auburn hair and freckles all over her soft pale skin. She had always been slightly eccentric with what she wore and was now wearing a thick, woolly jumper with reindeers on it, black tights, dancing socks and trainers. I had always loved her fashion sense.

Inside, the pub was warm and smelled of mulled wine. We walked into the wall of hot air. A table of friendly men on a stag do greeted us. Lizzy started waving and flirting with all of them. She was so inspiring. One of them was tall, with smooth, black skin and was dressed far better than the rest of them. He had his eye on Alysha who was playfully teasing him. I, on the other hand, became shy and looked at the floor. A couple of them were staring at me, but smiling enough that I didn't feel awkward.

"Can I get you ladies a drink?" One of the more handsome guys called over to us. He was leaning on the bar as he spoke. I went bright red. I felt so... included. Lizzy ordered us all sparkling rosé, and then, bottle in hand, she suddenly turned and proceeded upstairs. The boys seemed dumbstruck. Alysha was laughing with her new friend, but slinked away when she realised what Lizzy was doing. She grabbed my hand and pulled me along.

"Come on B" Alysha said, following Lizzy.

"Oh, charming ladies. Can't you stay?" One of the other guys said, laughing along with the others.

"Maybe when we finish this bottle, lads," flirted Alysha.

"Oh, I like her, you go girl!" Lizzy called down to Alysha as she continued up the stairs further. I felt like one of them. I felt normal. It was amazing. Could the guys at the bar tell? Probably. But I didn't care. It was all over before I had any time to worry.

The ice bucket hit the table, followed by three chilled champagne glasses. We all sat around the table. I could see outside, the streets were still full of shoppers hurrying home.

"So. You. Tell me everything." With a satisfied look on her face, Lizzy poured the rosé as we settled into our chairs.

"What on earth do you mean, Lizzy?" We all laughed. As if it wasn't obvious.

"Very funny. I remember when we were younger, you always used to talk about doing it. Look at you now... I'm so happy for you!" Lizzy took a swig of her sparkling pink rosé and I could tell she was tearing up a little. I got the sense that she had already been drinking for a bit. The cosy lighting of the pub made it easy to relax, and open up.

"Of course, I always knew it was something I wanted to do. It just got to the stage where it was something I had to do. I couldn't live life as a man anymore." Lizzy leaned in as if she had a million questions to ask me. But it didn't feel threatening. I could tell she was just interested. Happy for me. Maybe even proud of me?

"Well, good for you! So, when exactly did you decide? Ya' know... to transition?"

"It's been around eight months now. I just decided one day that the old me couldn't live anymore. Some shit went down and I ended up in hospital, but basically from that point I was reborn. It's like I was a phoenix rising up from the ashes or something epic like that. Like a butterfly."

"You were always unhappy as a boy. Even as a gay guy you were different. I had plenty of gay friends, but even they all could tell you were different." Lizzy revealed. I found it weirdly affirming to know that though. Alysha was listening to everything, taking it all in, and had already finished her glass. She helped herself to another and topped up mine and Lizzy's glasses. Alysha had only known me as a woman, as the new me, the real me, so this must have all been slightly bizarre for her.

"I remember asking for Barbie dolls as a kid, taking dance lessons, and trying on my mum's shoes... The signs were definitely there early on." We all laughed. Lizzy even snorted a little.

"So, what do I call you now? I take it you've changed your name, right? Have you started on hormones?" Lizzy asked. She knew a lot more about the process than I expected.

"I changed my name by deed poll around a month ago. My name is officially Fiona White, but everyone calls me Beam, which is a nickname I used before deciding on my girl's name."

"Aww, both are totally cute. Fiona really suits you!" Lizzy smiled. She raised her glass up in front of her and leaned back in her chair. Alysha did the same. "Here's to you Fiona. Congratulations for following your dreams and being who you always wanted to be. I really am so happy for you!" Our glasses clinked and the sound made me smile. Lizzy downed it in one and grabbed the ice bucket.

"I'll go try and flirt our way into a second bottle!" She said as she giggled, and strutted down stairs.

The campfire was swamped in a pool of rainwater. Summer heat made the air humid and heavy. The storm brought harsh winds and thick, grey clouds. The purple sky had turned dark and ominous. Lightning flashed and thunder roared. Waves along the small beach on the Volcano Island were crashing violently against the ship. The crew had almost finished repairing it as best they could, and they were huddled below deck to get out of the rain. The Four Guardians were taking shelter under the trees next to the small beach, and were discussing whether or not they should go into the woods to look for Prince Hikaru and Queen Fubuki.

"Our orders were clear. We wait. No doubt the Queen cast a spell on us to sleep for so many moons, only she has that kind of power," reasoned Endurance.

"But why would she do that? We've been asleep for too long! Was it just us? What if she was hurt and that's why everything stopped," Defence argued. He despised the thought of the Queen getting hurt.

"How do we even know the world froze for six moons? Yes, it seems to be Summer now, but that doesn't mean we slept for all that time. Perhaps the Queen used her powers to bring about this season," said Strength. He was clearly trying to comfort Endurance, whom he had his arms around as they huddled under the leaves.

Before they were able to understand the peculiar situation they were in, they heard the sound of Kaze galloping through the woods, along the mystic path, and towards the small beach. Upon Kaze, rode Prince Hikaru and Queen Fubuki. Her hair was clinging to her face and neck. The rain was lashing down on them, but they rode on anyway.

"My Queen!" Strength screamed.

"Queen Fubuki" Defence fell to one knee. The others bowed their heads.

"My Guardians, I am glad to see you have come to no harm. Rise, let me see you." Queen Fubuki jumped from her horse and walked over to Defence. She lifted his chin and he stood up slowly. Prince Hikaru slid off Kaze and walked him towards the ship. The crew, hearing something going on outside, had started to climb out onto the upper deck.

"What happened? Is everything alright, my Queen?" Agility asked hastily.

"I found the evil that attacked our people. He called himself the King of Truth. Deep within the woods he attacked me and we had a great battle. We must find him and stop him. He is strong, but when we gather our strength we will be strong enough to defeat him. He wants to claim Macha Land for himself."

"He can't!" Defence burst out.

"No, and he won't. We will destroy him! We will protect the people of Macha Land!" Queen Fubuki raised her head and looked at her Guardians through the heavy rainfall. They smiled with joy and each drew their weapon of choice. In unison, they cheered for her. The rain danced off their armour and weapons. But they cheered. They roared. They were hers until death.

"My Queen, the crew have tried to fix the ship, will you take a look?" Strength said gently.

"The ship? Why? What happened to it?" Queen Fubuki looked puzzled.

"There was a… an attack. Not the King of Truth, but a large sea monster. Not half a day after leaving the Bridge Over the River, we found ourselves fighting this great beast. The ship was damaged badly, and if it had not been for Agility, I would certainly not have made it here to you. The beast dragged me down into the depths of the sea after I tried to kill it." Prince Hikaru explained.

Fubuki went silent. It was as she had seen in the cauldron. Prince Hikaru surrounded by water and trapped with the woods. Why? Why was he being tested?

"I see. That is... most terrible. Is anyone hurt? How can I help?"

One of the crewmembers worked up enough confidence to address her directly. "No one is hurt, my Queen. But... the ship... may I ask that you cast a spell to finish repairing it?" His hands were trembling with nerves just from looking upon her dark black hair and beautiful face.

"Of course, my friend." She replied, smiling. "At once."

As Queen Fubuki walked over to the ship, with her subjects behind her, she saw Prince Hikaru approaching her. He looked worried.

"Fubuki, are you well enough to cast a spell?" He whispered into her ear. Her eyes widened – he rarely addressed her without honorifics. He must have been extremely concerned.

"This must be done. I will rest afterwards. Hikaru, I must tell you of my vision quest. When we set sail, visit me in my sleeping quarters." She did her best to keep herself confident and calm, when deep down she was just as worried as Hikaru. Never had she been defeated and so drained of her energies.

"Also, my Queen, if you want us to set sail without delay, may we ask that you clear this storm for us?" The crewmember asked, feeling more confident than before. Queen Fubuki looked at Hikaru, and then at the crewmember.

"I will repair the ship, but I may not be able to bring this storm to an end. It is a sign from the Goddess that we must sail with caution." The storm seemed worse in the direction of the Main Island. "Can you sail around it, rather than through it? Sail East, towards the second island. Then sail home from there, to the Southern Desert." She also wanted to avoid the creature in the sea. She didn't have enough magickal energy to halt this great storm, let alone fight that beast as well. Suddenly, a thought occurred to her. It was Summer. They would be sailing to the South of the Main Island. What of the Veil of Warmth? Winter had ended as she fell into her slumber, and Spring had begun. Spring had turned to Summer, and yet Fubuki had still not withdrawn the Veil of Warmth. A sharp pang of fear hit her as she contemplated what might have become of her island. She had to get home, as fast as she could.

If only she was strong enough to turn into her Phoenix form. She had tried once after waking, but her powers were depleted. Her people could be suffering, and she was helpless to stop it. For now, all she could do was repair the ship and sail home. Her crew were the best in the land. They would get her there as soon as they could. Prince Hikaru would be with her, which made her stronger. Everything would surely be fine.

Queen Fubuki stood in front of the ship, while the others stood behind her. Her feet were shoulder width apart and her arms outstretched, palms to the sky. Her dirty clothes flowed in the stormy winds, and the rain continued to fall on her. But she wouldn't be discouraged. She had to repair the ship.

"With wood as strong as metal,
And metal held into place,
Sail swift as a breeze blown petal,
All broken parts I now replace."

With her spell, the ship jolted upwards, as if three times lighter. Parts of the wooden frame started to come apart and danced around. There were creaks and cracks, and crunching sounds as the ship repaired itself. After the spell was complete, the ship fell back into the sea with a thud, sending waves right up to her feet. Fubuki could feel herself weaken. If she were alone, she would have fallen to the sand. But she had to be strong. She had to get home.

Everyone clambered onto the ship. The crew set sail immediately, heading East to avoid the heart of the storm. The Four Guardians guided the Queen below deck and then returned to keep watch above it. The rain lashed violently at their faces, but they had to stay alert. Prince Hikaru took Kaze down to the ship stables to keep him safe. He stayed to feed and clean him. Queen Fubuki found her sleeping chambers and sat quietly on the bed. She could finally let herself be tired. She closed her eyes and focused on healing.

When she opened her eyes, the storm could barely be heard anymore. She looked out the window and glimpsed the second largest island of Macha Land in the distance. It was still far away, but grew closer as the bow sliced through the waves. The heat made her want to remove her gowns and conjure an outfit better suited to the weather. But she decided she would wait before casting any more spells, and for now, she just stripped down to cool off. Her current clothes were far too dirty to wear anyway.

She heard three knocks on the door.

"My Queen, are you well?" Prince Hikaru called through the closed door.

"I'm awake now. Please enter." She replied. She was laying there naked with only a small roll of silk covering her from his gaze. He had also taken off his linens to wash the horse and was almost skyclad. Only his linen shorts covered him.

"Have you been resting?"

"Yes, and I feel better. I'm not completely back to full health, but I am better." His eyes were on her breasts.

"That's good." He walked over to her, and kneeled by the end of her bed.

His hair was loose and wet. His eyes were wide and full of emotion. She lay there, showing her legs and hips off to him. They looked at each other, locked in a gaze of lust. He leaned forward and reached out his

94

hands, pulling her lips onto his. Her breasts were firm as he caressed them. She closed her legs around his back and they fell onto the bed together. Both of them were excited by their journey together and the adventure they were on. The boat rocked at a steady pace with the sea. They were in harmony with each other. The sun shone through the ship windows onto her bed sheets. He could feel the heat from the sun on his back as he took her.

He entered her whilst his eyes looked deep into hers. He dared not look away. She dug her nails into him. They were connected. They were in love. They were the only two beings in the world that mattered. She moaned as he continued to pleasure her. They kissed. He groaned. She screamed. Until it was too much for him and brought him to release. He rolled over, but he needed to be close to her, so he pulled her into his arms. His hand wrapped around her stomach and pulled her effortlessly across the bed. She slid over, and giggled as he held her tightly from behind. Even after finishing, he still wished he was kissing her. They were in love. They always would be, in life and in death.

Above deck, a crewmember shouted something that was muffled by the wind. Hikaru held her close, as she snuggled into him. From the window she could see that land was almost close enough to anchor the ship. They would have to leave their paradise eventually to continue their voyage home.

"Let's get dressed, we will be needed soon." He whispered into her ear. She nodded silently, cherishing his embrace. They stood up, and he grabbed his linens from the floor by her bed. Fubuki looked at her dirty outfit in a heap on the floor. That just wouldn't do. With a click of her fingers she summoned her golden staff from thin air. Hikaru looked back at her, surprised.

"I'm back to my normal self, my love. My energy, it's back. I feel... stronger." She smiled and with a wave of her staff, she emitted a bright red light. Red slithers of electricity pulsed up and down her body. In a flash of brilliant red light, she was done. Her body was covered in a vermillion gown. Sophisticated and comfortable. It was perfect for Summer. It had long sleeves, which was typical of her gowns, but the upper part of the dress was a light, silky fabric. The skirt of the gown was made of a net material, which was just thick enough to cover her. Her curvy figure still made her Prince burn with desire. Her hair had broken free from her bun and now flowed down in loose, dark waves. So much so that her thin nose and eyes were hidden in them.

She ascended to the upper deck, as the crew found a cove to anchor in. They tied a rope to shore and secured a plank for their Queen to walk down. They had decided to rest here for the night, as the crew's strength was still depleted. The Main Island could be seen ever so faintly in the distance. It wouldn't be long before they were home.

Queen Fubuki was still worried about the Veil of Warmth. She couldn't see the island well enough, but she hoped against hope that it had been taken down at the end of Winter. Everyone had been frozen in time, but perhaps the Coven of Rosemary had somehow taken it down now? She could only hope. She dreaded to think what it would be like in Summer with the Veil still in place. Surely there would be a drought and her people would be suffering.

With her staff still in her hand, she walked down the wooden plank to the shallow water. It was the clearest, purest water she had ever seen. The sun blazed down on her. A soft breeze was in the air, cooling her skin ever so gently. She heard Kaze trot down the plank behind her, led by Hikaru, and the others followed shortly after. The sandy shores were all she could see on either side. Nothing but sand. She looked back at her Prince, as if to check on him. He nodded slowly.

"I am taking Kaze for a while. I haven't ridden him for some time now." She declared. She felt powerful now, and that power made her feel safe. She felt more connected to the Goddess than ever.

"As you wish, my Queen." Prince Hikaru guided Kaze to her and she straddled him instantly. But before she could settle comfortably on her horse, he leapt up in fright. Fubuki was launched backwards into the air and quickly levitated herself before hitting the floor. Her slippers fell away from her, leaving her barefoot. As she landed she felt the sand between her toes. She felt suddenly connected to the island. Kaze galloped back to the ship and Hikaru went chasing after him. But Queen Fubuki stayed where she was. She was rooted in the ground. She could feel the mass of dust and sand beneath her. Her eyes went black and within her mind's eye, she saw deep into the island. So much sand, earth and stone. Why did it feel so alive? This place was nothing more than a wasteland.

Then suddenly, she felt it. Deep beneath the sand, she felt the gaping void. The darkness. Then she felt the black fire. The evil flames. The burning. He was here. She could feel him. The King of Truth was here. He was surrounded by thousands of small, twisted creatures, with pointy claws and heads made of hard shell that were shaped like upturned shields. They were chained together in lines. Forced to work and move in unison. All she could hear was the clang of metal against metal. Screams. Cries. She saw fire melting everything in its path. Her visions were horrible. Dark. It reeked of death.

"This place is not safe, we must leave at once". She shouted behind her. She could finally see normally again. She started running for the ship. The others boarded without a word of argument. Her tone did nothing to invite it. The darkness she had felt was still with her. Still inside her. It pulled her down like a rock. As she made her way back up the plank, she heard the same crackle of black lightning behind her that she had heard on the Volcano Island. It was him.

"For six moons the Queen slumbers and forgets her people. The blistering heat consumes them. The cursed kiss of the Phoenix... how ironic. What a waste. What a pity. I thought you a better ruler. No matter... I will take your realm for my own and your precious island will know fire like it has never known before."

Prince Hikaru drew Winter's Dagger at once and went to face the King head on. Queen Fubuki stopped him with magick and moved towards the King. She knew her Prince was no match for this evil. His words alone had made her feel sick. His voice was like poison bleeding into her ears.

"You speak as if you know fire? Then burn." She screamed at him. Her wings spread out beside her, forcing Hikaru to step back. The Four Guardians stood back in awe of her, as she grew to three times her size. Her red and orange feathers sprouted and caught alight. Flames shot from her glowing beak and went straight for the King of Truth. He dodged them by teleporting into his black lightning, until she covered the area with so much fire that he had no place to go. The heat raged on as she covered herself in the same flames.

Within seconds she was back in her human form. Her red robe was scorched and charred. Running towards him with her staff, she whirled it in his direction while he was still consumed in the flames. Suddenly, from behind her, a small tidal wave reached over and engulfed him. The flames went out with a hiss. She watched him struggle to breathe. The water spiralled upwards like a tornado of liquid. Then she held her staff still in the air and blew gently onto it. The breath turned to a breeze, and the breeze to a gale. Soon it felt like a hurricane was upon them all. The ship began to lurch violently. The crew held on tight to anything they could reach. Kaze bucked. Defence span around and thrust his shield into the ground. The Four Guardians and the Prince moved behind it instantly.

As the watery tornado enveloped the evil King, he waved his hand and the tornado turned black. Blades of black lightning hit everything around him. Some bolts caught the ship, which started to smoke. With this, Fubuki knelt on the floor, her palms touching the sand.

"Consume him," she whispered. The sands began to move. The floor gave way. In a flash, the black swirling vortex was eaten up by the island. Soon he would return back down to his deep, dark pit of hatred.

They wasted no time getting back to the ship. Mere moments later, the crew was ready to sail away and everyone was aboard. Everyone, except for Queen Fubuki. She had developed a taste for the fight and now all she wanted to do was hunt him down. However, she knew she couldn't take on his army of twisted creatures and monsters as well. She would need an army herself. She also had to get back to her island and make sure her people were safe. It had been too long.

"Hikaru!" She called to him, but he just beckoned her to board the ship. "Go, sail to the Southern Desert. I will fly home and withdraw the Veil of Warmth as soon as I can." Her voice was strong and clear. "I cannot wait for the ship."

"I will not leave you again, Fubuki!" Prince Hikaru dared to shout back at her. His love for her clouded his better judgement. The crew looked up in fear for him. But Queen Fubuki just smiled.

"My dear Prince, you have little choice…"

With her golden staff in hand, she faced the ship. She began to spin it between both hands, around and around. Wind began to blow and lifted her off of the floor. Her outfit fell apart into hundreds of red ribbons that swirled around her. She stopped, faced the ship again, and thrust her arms out in front of her. The ribbons were taken with a great gust of wind that only strengthened the closer it got to the ship. The waves beneath stirred. The ship began to move. The red ribbons circled the ship magnificently. The winds filled the sails so quickly that the crew could barely keep up. The boat began to soar along, cutting through the waves. Everyone held on tight, as it sped through the water.

Fubuki wasted no time and in a flash of fire, she was in the air. She was the Phoenix and she ascended to the skies. Graceful and determined. Flawless. Her wings snapped as she flew through the air. Before long she would be back at the Main Island. Home. Soon she would withdraw the Veil of Warmth, save her people and prepare for the fiercest battle Macha Land had ever seen.

When I was a boy I was called Eric. Eric White. My parents named me assuming that my gender was correctly assigned at birth and that I would always be a boy. I wouldn't. From early on my family could see that I wasn't happy. It was clear that I didn't want to act like boys did. I didn't want to be a boy at all. But it would be a long time before my family and I realised exactly what that meant. It took years for me to understand that I should have been born Fiona instead of Eric.

I remember asking for a Barbie doll at Christmas. For a couple of years, I got things like Action Men or toy cars. I played with them because I didn't want to look ungrateful, but eventually I got my way. I kept asking for girls' toys, until no one could deny me any longer. The first thing I bought with my pocket money was a Barbie doll. She had long hair and I made her all sorts of outfits. My mother taught me how to sew, and I made long dresses by hand for my doll. I wrapped my Action Men dolls in insulating tape to make them look like ninjas. The Barbie would be in charge. She would be a magical witch or a powerful Princess.

I remember cutting one of my dolls' hair, which didn't work very well. It didn't keep its shape and went all spikey at the back. I played with another doll in the bath, pretending she was a mermaid. Her hair got all tangled and knotted after that. I must have gone through thousands by the time I was old enough to realise how unusual it was for little boys to want to play with little girls' toys. I didn't care though, I was different anyway. I knew that from a young age.

None of that really mattered until school started. I didn't really realise the difference between boys and girls before then. My parents were loving and accepting of me and probably thought I would grow up to be gay. But when I started school and the teachers started splitting up the class into "boys" and "girls", it suddenly felt wrong to me. Why wasn't I on the other side of the class?

I made friends, as any child tries to do. I did have male friends too, but most of my closer friends were girls. At break time, I would leave the boys to play football and "stuck in the mud", and go over to the girls who would be sitting, reading and chatting. Sometimes if the boys asked us, we would join in and play "stuck in the mud", but I was always on the girl's team. They were all so nice. They got to wear skirts, and socks with pretty patterns on them. I had to wear a baggy white shirt and long grey trousers. I felt bound in a sea of fabric. I wanted to wear what the other girls wore. Sometimes, I rolled my white socks down to try and match how the girls' socks flared out at the ankles.

Then I grew up a bit more and the other kids started to notice something was wrong me. They called me names and even bullied me. It didn't help when my female friends stuck up for me and fought off the bullies. That only made things worse. It was around then that I started to analyse myself and finally started to understand just how different I actually was.

"It's like, if you were in your mummy's belly, and you had to press buttons." I would explain. I was in the canteen with my friends, eating instant mash potato and cold spaghetti hoops. We were so young that the dinner ladies would help us carry our drinks to the tables, otherwise we would have spilt them.

"What do you mean Eric?" Becky asked.

"There are no buttons on my mummy, are there on yours?" Sarah said sarcastically.

"No, no, they are not real buttons, silly! It's like, if you pressed buttons to make you a boy or a girl. Then more buttons to make your brain a boy's brain or a girl's brain." They nodded as they listened. "It's like I pressed the button to get a boy's body, but pressed the other button and got a girl's brain."

"Eugh, brains are gross," Abby said, laughing and snorting. We all laughed, brains *were* pretty gross.

It went on like this for years. I was bullied because the world around me thought I was an effeminate and gay boy. Luckily, I had my friends to protect me. When I came home from school, I didn't think about it as much. My family were kind and accepting of whatever or whoever I was. I was lucky there. It was just school that was the problem. Unfortunately, things only got worse as I grew up.

* * *

It was 10 a.m., on a Tuesday in South London. It must have been winter, because as I remember we were wrapped up in our coats and boots. I was in Year 5 now, at a primary school in Kent. I must have been around 10. With the rest of my classmates, we used to go to the local swimming pool. Going on the coach each week was so much fun. I was starting to become more self-aware by then. My friends and I would pair up in a line and make our way to the school bus. I always wanted to sit next to my best friend, Maria. Sometimes I would sit with Sarah, and that was ok.

At the time, the journey seemed to take hours, when in actual fact it was only down the road. Just leaving school grounds was enough excitement for the entire class, let alone the swimming lessons that we were taking. The other girls and I would talk about everyday things, who fancied who, what we had for lunch and which teacher we hated the most. Those few minutes were perfect. It was like the bus was a safe haven. Not school, but not completely removed from school life either.

Then the bus pulled into the swimming pool car park. The engine stopped running and the bus came to a halt. As soon as the teacher started to take the register, a sense of dread washed over me. It had begun.

Sarah and the other girls ran off with the female teacher, and I was left with Mr Chapman. The boys of the class continued their casual chats while I sat there silently on my own. Some of the nicer ones tried to include me, but it didn't help. I could already tell by then that something felt fundamentally and drastically wrong with me.

We huddled together under the supervision of the male teacher, and my heart began to sink. The comments started. Young children can say the harshest of things. Perhaps they didn't even understand what they were saying. Looking back, I would like to believe that. The teacher – of course oblivious to all of this – went about his role of ensuring that we all ended up safely in the right place. Around forty young boys were herded into the small swimming pool changing rooms.

Instinctively, I scurried away to the furthest corner, away from everyone. I had my swimming trunks ready underneath my boy's uniform, ready for a quick change, so I could make a swift escape to my friends on the other side of the wall. But it just was not that easy.

"Don't look Eric, you gay boy!"

"Yeah, GAY BOY! Hey guys, don't let Eric see your dick, he'll grab it!"

With my eyes fixed on the floor and my face covered by my hands, I only made it worse by acting suspicious and awkward. I just about managed to hold back the tears. Even then, I understood how catastrophic it would have been to start crying. Instead, I pretended to ignore everything and got changed as fast as my little arms allowed. I bolted out of the changing rooms, past the bullies and made my way to my friends.

Maria, and the other girls, Abby, Charlotte and Sarah eventually made their way out of the female changing rooms. The female teacher had gotten used to meeting me there each time and held my hand whilst we walked to the swimming pool. For that slight moment the pain of being bullied went away and I was who I was meant to be. I was with my friends, being looked after by the female teacher, whose smile was as soft as sunshine on a Sunday morning. She spoke to me as if she understood everything. Her brown hair, tied up in a ponytail, came down behind her shoulders.

"Are you ok? Ready for a swim?"

"Yes, miss. Thank you, miss."

I remember how she would always smile so sweetly. My hand still held tightly in hers, it was almost like she understood everything, years before even I did. It was as if she knew that I was meant to be one of the girls in the class. She made me feel safe. A safety that I had yet to feel at school. She seemed to know me better than I knew myself.

Unfortunately, she was as powerless as I was. I failed to grasp how to do the breast stroke and the backwards stroke in swimming class, and after the hour long lesson we all made our way back to the changing rooms. Then the exact same thing would happen. The boys would call me names, push me around and make me feel terrible. What was worse this time, was the fact that I had to take off my swimming trunks and put on my pants. I had no way of preventing that. No one did.

All I could do was look up. The ceiling was my sanctuary. I got changed whilst holding back tears, whilst the entire class laughed at me. I didn't want to see their genitals and I didn't want them to see mine. So all I could do was hide away in the height of the ceiling. Soon I would be back on that bus, with my friends. Maria, Sarah and the rest of them. Soon we would be talking together and I would be happy.

A few years later, when I was old enough to come home from school on my own, I remember listening to music on my Walkman and drifting off into a fantasy world. I mainly listened to female artists like Britney Spears, Samantha Mumba and B*Witched. It wasn't a long walk home, but I would take my time and enjoy the freedom.

It was the only time I could escape from everything. When I was walking forward, I couldn't see my face. I couldn't see my body. I could be whatever I wanted to be. I started to imagine a female character who would walk along too. She didn't have a name. She was a part of me. She *was* me. I imagined myself as her, walking along. Her hair would flow in the wind, and we would walk along to the music. I didn't realise back then how much I wanted to be her, but I remember her existence very well. One day, I would make the choice to become her.

Until then, I would have to deal with the pain and the turmoil. I didn't understand why I had to go through this. Was it only me? I felt so alone and confused. I wasn't able to express my inner turmoil clearly to the people around me. At that time, I didn't even know why I felt so confused. I didn't know about gender identity or gender dysphoria. Now I know that it was because I was meant to be a woman in this world. This of course was no one's fault, but it was a problem that I would have to live with until I grew old enough to take action. It would eventually consume me, and the fear of living forever as a man led me to take my own life as "Eric". I would then be reborn as the woman I should always have been. Reborn as her. Reborn as Fiona.

"Hi there gentlemen, what seems to be the problem?" I said to the group of six sitting at table twelve.

"Oh look, it's Mrs Doubtfire." They roared with laughter. That was pretty original. I forced a smile.

"We waited nearly an hour to be seated and now we've been waiting another hour for our food. Where is it?" One of the more sober members of the party said.

"I know. I apologise for the wait for the table. We recommend booking for a table of six on a Friday night. I have checked with the head chef about your food, it's being served up as we speak. Again, I'm very sorry – an hour is far too long to wait. Shall I see what I can do about a free bottle of wine for your table?" I said calmly.

Those idiots should have booked anyway.

"That seems fair. Yes. Thank you."

"Yeah, thanks Boy George." The other piped up again. A couple were polite enough to hold in their laughter, but smiles crept over their faces.

"Thank you for understanding. I will have one brought to your table. Also, here is our card with our contact details. Please do book with us to ensure you get seated faster at peak times. I hope you enjoy the rest of your evening, gentlemen." I was used to the jokes by now. They bounced off me like I was wearing armour. Some I genuinely laughed along with. It's good to be open. Honest. This group was just made up of idiots though. They were too loud and moaned about everything.

Ellie was the new girl and was assigned to their table, but couldn't really handle them. Fair enough, they were a handful. I walked into the back area, and was marking off food for another table when she came up behind me.

"Fiona, thank you so much! How did you get them to calm down? I felt so intimidated by them." The poor girl looked genuinely scared.

107

"They're just drunk. They need a firm hand. Talk to them with 50% flirtation to get their attention, and 50% as if you're their mother. That's the only way to get through to them. They're just bastards." I wanted her to feel better. I didn't know where that anger came from though.

"Right! They totally are! Don't come on a Friday, without booking, and expect a table for six!"

"Exactly!" We laughed together. "Hun, can you take this to table twenty?"

"Sure... table twenty is..."

"Upstairs, to your right." I pointed towards the stairs.

"Upstairs! Thank you!" Ellie left with the plates. She could only take two at a time, which slowed her down. I was about to follow her with four, when Alysha came through with dirty ones.

"Hey girl, you good?" She asked, smiling.

"I'm good. Rockin' it as always. You?" I said, walking past, smiling.

"Saw you dealt with twelve." She meant the table. She must have seen.

"Yeah, they weren't that bad."

"Don't let them talk to you like that though B. Paul said to tell him if you get any abuse and he will kick them out." Alysha said quietly to me, holding my arm. She was such a kind girl. I loved her so much.

"You're too cute, Alysha. Thank you. It's honestly fine. I'm a bitch when I'm drunk too, I can't judge them for that. Plus my hair is all short and stuff, maybe I kinda do look like Mrs Doubtfire." I laughed. She couldn't hold in a giggle either.

It was busy, so I had to go. I served table twenty their food with a smile. Paul was at the main counter, so I asked about the free bottle of house wine for the table of idiots, and he nodded. Alysha must have spoken to him, because he knew about everything. I went upstairs to check on Ellie and generally take another look. It was busy, even for a Friday. Surprising considering it was January. Then I realised it was late January, so people had started to get paid this month. That explained it.

Back downstairs, I cleared a couple of tables as I made my way back into the kitchen. I noticed table twelve had their wine now, and were calming down a bit. Still no food though. That's not good. Chef looked very stressed, and no one dared approach him. I noticed a pile of onions that needed chopping, where one of the new chefs had been. Without a word, I put the dirty plates into the dishwasher and washed my hands.

"Fiona, what are you doing?" The chef asked.

"Can I just help for a bit, take a break from the floor?" He was running behind, surely he would let me. As of a month ago, I had a level 1 certificate in food safety and hygiene. I was allowed to handle food and help with basic prep.

"Ok. Just no mess!" He shouted, then carried on cooking. He actually seemed a little bit relieved.

The rest of the shift went by, and most customers went home satisfied. I pushed Ellie to upsell desserts to table twelve, even though a table of men like that rarely ordered desserts. But she did, so the revenue would cover the bottle of wine. Chef went home after last orders, and got the rest of his team to clean up. Alysha and I went down to get changed. There were still five people working on the floor upstairs, but Alysha and I had worked a double shift so were told to finish for the day.

"What a night! Still, not too late. Any plans B?" Alysha asked, throwing on her boyfriend's hoodie over her uniform top.

"No, no plans. Ice cream and chill until I fall asleep." I just wanted to be in bed.

"Sounds good. You ready?"

"Yeah, ready." I didn't take my makeup off anymore. My hair was getting longer, and I was passing more and more each day. It was winter, so I could wrap myself in a scarf and keep my head down if I felt in danger. But generally, people didn't notice me in the dark. Generally.

Alysha had taught me how to contour my face and we had been on a makeup shopping trip in the January sales. Since then, my makeup had been a hundred times better. That helped my confidence, which meant I smiled more. Everyone said that I looked better when I was smiling. It was great. I was really starting to see changes within myself.

As Alysha and I walked up the stairs from the staff room, I could see Paul by the tills. He taught me how to cash up a while ago, in case he was ever ill. I guess I was now his second in command, which was crazy, as I hadn't been there very long. Alysha was great, but I don't think Paul liked her as much. She wasn't very serious.

"Erm... Hi!" I turned around. A guy had stood up from his table and walked over to me. Alysha turned around too.

"Hi?" I said, confused. Then I recognised him. "Oh my god, Karl!?" It was Karl Stevenson! He was my closest friend through secondary school, before Georgina. I hadn't seen him in years. Not since... before.

"Is that really you? You look amazing! I'm... I'm so proud of you." Karl was slightly drunk, and had always had a bit of a stutter. He had short black hair and deep blue eyes. In secondary school, he was kind of an emo and let his hair grow out. But now it was cut short and really suited him. He looked incredible actually. I remember we used to listen to rock music together, and he knew all the lyrics to every song.

"Yeah, it's me. My name's Fiona now." I smiled. I wanted to talk more. I wanted to hug him there and then, but everyone was watching.

"Fiona, hi. That's a pretty name. Wow, this is incredible. It's so good to see you. Listen, we should go for drinks." He seemed genuine.

"Sure! That would be nice. I ran into Lizzy about a month ago, you knew Lizzy right?"

"Yes! Lizzy! I remember! What a flashback, wow." He was lost in his memories. He was always cute when he was drunk.

"Ok, well I have to go, I'll add you ok? I have a new profile now."

"Oh, of course. Right, ok. Cool! Have a good night then ladies." He said to both me and Alysha.

We walked out, saying bye to Paul as we went. He was still counting so he raised a hand until he finished the pile of notes he was on and finally looked up at us.

"Good work tonight girls, especially you Fiona. Nicely done with table twelve." Paul waved and started counting a different pile of notes.

As we walked along together, I was tempted to ask Alysha if she had time for a drink, as it was early. But I was tired, and one drink always led to three.

"Hun, I would say let's go for a drink, but I'm so tired. Tomorrow night, yeah?" I said, being honest.

"Girl, you read my mind. Totally. Sleep tight boo!" She walked off towards the tube. My bus arrived just as I got to the bus stop. I wrapped myself in my scarf, put my headphones in and sat there quietly. I could feel that winter was coming to an end and soon it would be spring. I missed the heat of summer, but I was worried about what I would do. It's not like I would be confident enough to walk around in crop tops and summer dresses. But there was no point worrying about that just yet.

When I got home I found a note on my door from Georgina.

Out for the night, love you!

Fair enough. I was excited to tell her that I had run into Karl, but it could wait until tomorrow. I went to the kitchen, grabbed a tub of ice cream and took it to my room. I threw my bag down by my bed, stripped off my coat, clothes and underwear and quickly jumped into my pyjamas. It was cold as the heating hadn't been on, so I slipped straight into bed. As funny cats fell over on YouTube, I started at the ice cream and took off my make-up with a facial wipe. Tomorrow was the day I had to change my hormone patch, so I set one out for myself. If I overslept I would probably go to work without it on, and that would mess up my schedule.

I was checking my phone when I noticed something. Karl had found my profile and added me. How sweet. He must have looked me up on his way home. I was surprised he even remembered my new name. I accepted, then put my phone back down on the bedside table. Then the screen flashed again. He had messaged me. Already.

Hi Fiona, nice to see you again. You look really happy! All the best, Karl.

Aww, that was so sweet. We were best friends in school. He was my only male friend. I always felt sorry for him, because everyone thought he was gay. Once when I was at a family party at his house, his mum got drunk and started talking to me. She poured me a glass of white wine (even though I must have been about fifteen) and looked me straight in the eyes.

"You are a great person. My son would be lucky to have you. Whatever he is, I accept him," she said, and she clearly meant it. What a cool mum.

"Mrs Stevenson, it's honestly not like that. Karl and I are just really good friends. He looks out for me." I smiled at her and sipped my wine. It tasted nice. I could tell it was expensive.

"Oh, so my boy isn't good enough for you then?" She joked and burst out laughing. She was slightly eccentric, but also the coolest mum ever.

I stared at my phone, remembering all the good times we had. I used to be in love with him. Of course I was. I had been since the first time I set eyes on him in our class room, back in year 8. He was one of the cool kids and yet kept his independent personality and style. I continued to love him, for many years. But I hadn't lied to his mother that day. We had never been a couple. We were just friends. Back then I was a different person completely. Back then I was Eric.

I was too tired to reply to his message and also it didn't leave much room to reply. I decided I would finish my ice cream, brush my teeth and then go to sleep. I would think of something to say to Karl in the morning. Plus, I had to be up for work early. That night I had my usual dreams of a faraway world, about a Queen and her Prince.

* * *

The following morning I woke up late as usual. I managed to remember my patch that I had set out the night before. I had been on hormones for nearly a year now and I was starting to see things changing. Slowly but surely, my body fat was changing. My bum was getting bigger and rounder. My hips were larger and my skin was softer.

I remember the day I realised that my breasts were coming through. I was lounging around the house with Georgina on a Sunday and she randomly pointed at my chest. I looked down and saw my nipples were fighting their way through my pyjamas. At that point, I realised that the hormones were really working and we rolled around on the sofa laughing for about ten minutes. It was magical. From that day onwards, I never needed to use chicken fillets again.

On the bus, I was checking my contouring was ok when I remembered Karl's message. I hadn't even replied yet. I read it again, and decided to reply before I got to work. *Hi Fiona, nice to see you again. You look really happy! All the best, Karl.* Well yes, I was happy.

It was also really nice to see him again. But "all the best" was difficult to reply to. I sat and thought for a moment. A woman gave me a strange look and sat towards the back of the bus. I must not have been passing as a woman as well as I thought today. Oh well, back to the message.

Hey Karl, it really was good to see you. Hope all is well, Fiona x

Simple. Work was just around the corner, but my favourite song was playing on my phone. I wouldn't be able to finish listening to it by the time I got to the restaurant. I always hated it when that happened. Then he messaged me back.

Hey. I was worried you didn't get home safe or something. Are you working today? Fancy catching up over a drink?

I read it about three times. I couldn't help remembering back to when we were close friends. It would be really great to have him as a friend again. I felt so safe around him.

Sure! I'm working today, but only the lunch shift. I could meet you around 6? Obviously I'll be at the restaurant.

I only checked my reply twice. It sounded ok.

Awesome, I'll meet you at 6 when you finish (seems long for a lunch shift!) See you then!

I couldn't deny it, my heart was racing a bit. As one sided as it was, I had loved him once. He was the first guy I ever loved. Maybe a part of me would always love him. Either way, I had to turn my work brain on and forget about that for a while.

The lunch shift was usually easier than the evening shift, except on Saturdays. As far as the restaurant was concerned, there was no difference between lunch and dinner on the weekends. It was very busy and I barely had any time to think about Karl. It wasn't until around 5 p.m. that I started looking towards the entrance occasionally, to see if he turned up early. Alysha could tell something was on my mind, but we were too busy to talk about it.

I was checking my makeup and doing whatever I could to look feminine when she said something. She was working a double shift, so she didn't have much time to talk in the staff room. I smiled at her and said it was nothing important. When she worked out that I was meeting up with the guy who we'd seen at the restaurant she nearly exploded.

"Girl! Shit! Are you seeing him? Like a date?" She was so loud, I was worried the customers on the ground floor could hear her all the way down here in the basement.

"No! We're just going for a drink... as friends. Honestly, it's not like that. Who's going to be into a '*girl like me*?'" I laughed and pouted dramatically at her. She shook her head.

"Shut up B, you have no idea how beautiful you are. You are, like, beyond gender itself. You will find someone, for sure." She was high today, I could tell. Her pupils were the size of soup bowls.

Paul called down to Alysha, and she had to run up, pretending she had been in the stock room. I giggled as she randomly grabbed a large tin of tomatoes and frantically ran upstairs.

It was 6 p.m. so I walked upstairs and waved goodbye to Alysha who was taking a table order. Paul was walking back from serving table four.

"You off out Fiona?" He asked.

"Yes actually, just drinks with a friend." I smiled and waved to go.

"Ok, well, be safe, ok? See you tomorrow" he said and I watched him walk into the kitchen. He always seemed worried about me ever since the night that guy tried to assault me. He was like an older brother to me. We sometimes joked about how jealous I was that his hair was longer than mine.

Karl was waiting for me at the bar near the entrance of the restaurant. He had a beer in his hand and glass of white wine next to him. When he saw me he stood up and smiled.

"Hey you," he said.

"You ok?"

"Yeah, you? I didn't know how long you would be, so I got these." He showed me the beer in his hand and nodded towards the glass of wine on the bar.

"Thanks Karl, that's really sweet." I picked up the glass and clinked it against his bottle of beer. I took a long sip and savoured it. He remembered that I liked Pinot Grigio from secondary school. Behind me, Alysha was smiling and I noticed that even Paul was staring. I didn't understand what was so amusing. I told her we were just drinking as friends.

"So it looks like we have a lot of catching up to do... You're a woman now?" He said, as clear as day. I laughed into my wine glass at how frank he was being. There was no one close enough around us to hear him, but still it was embarrassing to hear him say it so abruptly.

"No... Whatever do you mean?" We laughed. "Yeah, no, I am. You knew me well back in secondary school, probably more than anyone. I always knew deep down, I just never let myself admit it."

"Yeah, that's true. To be honest, when I saw you, I wasn't shocked at all. I'm sure you mentioned it when we were mates before. It was more like 'Oh right, yeah, makes sense' in my head." He spoke calmly and honestly. It was surreal talking to him about it. "I bet it was hard though, coming out all over again."

"Yeah, it was at times. I always pretended to be 'the gay guy' because it was easier, but it got less easy over time". I took another large sip of my wine, as I noticed he was nearly finished with his beer. Also, I could still feel Alysha's eyes on me, so I was happy to leave as soon as possible.

116

"Well, you look stunning, it really suits you. I take it it's been a good few years?" He asked.

"Years? No! God no! It's been like, just over a year since I started hormones."

"What? Really? What are hormones?" He looked confused. It was sweet and I was happy to explain.

"Hormone replacement therapy. It basically sets the ground work for a female body. Your body basically goes through female puberty. It's started to work, but it's still early days." I looked down at myself and shrugged my shoulders.

"Well, I disagree. I mean, you can still tell... but you look more feminine than some normal girls I know." He meant it as a compliment, I was sure of it. But he could tell by my face that he had said something wrong. "Oh. Shit. I didn't mean that you aren't normal. Of course not. You are. Erm... so, what should I call a nor... a girl born as a girl then?"

"It's ok. I know you didn't mean it offensively. That would be a cis woman."

"Oh yeah, I've heard of that actually. Sweet. So yeah, you look more feminine than some cis women I know." He said, proud that he'd learnt a new word. "And also, I know a trans man. There's a guy at my work. He's really short and a bit chubby, but you wouldn't know unless he told you. We're good mates actually, he's a real laugh." He smiled as he explained it to me. He was trying to show how ok with it he was.

"That's cool. I've finished my wine now, shall we go somewhere else?" I grabbed my bag and put my coat on.

"Sure, let's go. Have you eaten?" He asked, looking down at me. He had always been slightly taller.

"Not yet and I'm starving actually." I really was. It had been a long day.

"Great, follow me, I know a good place."

He took me to a place in North London that was actually quite close to my flat. It was a Japanese sushi restaurant. Karl told me about travelling in Asia and that Japanese food was still his favourite. When we were younger we used to watch Japanese anime and talk about Asia a lot. It seemed like such an exotic place to us.

He was wearing a red shirt, with a black waistcoat and skinny jeans. His hair was cut very short on the sides and he had a fringe covering his face. He wasn't muscular, but because he was tall he still had a masculine frame. His jaw was defined and he seemed to be trying to grow a beard. It didn't suit him. On his right hand, he had a ring on his middle finger with a Celtic pattern on it that looked familiar.

We entered the restaurant. It was dark, but warm and cosy.

"Irasshaimase!" The staff called out in unison. One of the waitresses came over and asked how many people were in our party. Since working in a restaurant, I looked at other restaurants differently.

"Two of us, I have a reservation actually, under Stevenson." Karl said to the cute Japanese lady.

"Oh right, Mr Stevenson. This way please." She said, as she walked us to our table. It was a table for two on a raised platform area, with a wall of bamboo shielding us from the rest of the restaurant. I could see the fresh sushi and sashimi in the glass counter from the entrance. It was such a great place and it was really sweet of him to bring us here. He had even booked. I hid a smile of delight.

We had barely sat down and he was already ordering for us. I just sat there, impressed at his knowledge of the menu. He barely looked at it.

"Can we get two portions of yaki-gyoza, some edamame, and chicken kara-age. Then the sushi platter 3 for after." He looked up at me. "Does that sound ok?"

I had no idea.

"Sure! Sounds amazing."

"Great. And erm... she'll have a glass of Pinot Grigio and can I have a small Asahi please?"

The waitress bowed and went off to the kitchen.

"You must have had an amazing time travelling through Asia. I bet it really opened your eyes to the world." I said, almost in awe of him.

"Yeah, it was amazing. I experienced a lot. But everywhere you go, everyone's just... people. Ya' know? Like, we are all just the same people, going about our lives. Striving on." Wow... that was intense. I was slightly lost in his eyes when the waitress came over with our drinks. Very fast and both drinks were freezing cold. Impressive.

"Small Asahi for you, sir." She placed down a beer mat, and then the drink. "...and a glass of wine for the lady." I smiled. Then Karl noticed that my face had lit up and he smiled too. Then we chuckled between ourselves.

"Cheers. To you Fiona. For finally becoming yourself. Something most people take for granted." Our glasses clinked and I took a long gulp. It was delicious. Everything was.

We drank the night away, and enjoyed fresh fish, sticky rice and exotic desserts after that. We laughed a lot and talked about old times. He was sweet enough to refer to me using female pronouns, even when we were talking about me in the past. My family hadn't even managed that yet. Sometimes even Georgina slipped up. We talked about his mum and his family in general. We talked about our old school and the old friend group. Lizzy came up a lot, even though I never thought Karl and Lizzy were close. He knew Georgina too, but not very well.

I didn't realise how drunk I was until I stood up to go to the toilet. Then it hit me. But I still felt safe. The restaurant was busy and people were focused on their own tables. Normally I would be paranoid that everyone was staring at me, but the alcohol made me relax. That probably made me blend in more. I barely felt anyone's eyes on me at all. Except Karl's. He was watching me. Making sure I was ok. It was like having my old best friend back again. I had missed him a lot.

The waitress placed what I thought was the bill down on the table when I came back from the toilet. I went to grab my purse when Karl stopped me.

"It's fine, I've paid it. Don't be silly."

"What? Karl, no it's fine, let's split it."

"No, it's done. I've paid it already. This is just the receipt and the restaurant card. Here, take it." He gave me the card. It had a pretty Koi fish on it with Japanese symbols.

"Thank you Karl, I would have paid half..."

"Don't be silly. I wanted to treat you. Besides, you're a girl now. You have to get used to guys treating you like a princess."

"Karl, it's 2015. Not the fifties. Women pay for themselves too, ya' know." He grinned and nudged my shoulder gently like he did all those years ago. We went to leave when suddenly the staff shouted something at us again.

"Arigatou gozimashita!"

Then Karl turned to one of the staff bowing by the exit.

"Gochisousama." He said with a slight bow. When we got out of the restaurant I asked him what he'd said. Apparently it's what you're meant to say to thank someone for a meal. He talked about how he picked up quite a lot when he was travelling. He had really grown up. I imagined he would still be the drug taking teenager I remembered him to be. I guess we had both changed a lot. I smiled to myself.

"You ok, Fiona?"

"Oh, yeah, I was just thinking about how we have both changed so much. Ya' know, in our own little ways."

"Yeah, it's true. But we are still the same deep down. To me, you were always a girl. Well, deep down." He grinned his cheeky grin again.

"Well yeah, I was. I think we were such good friends because I knew you got it."

"Yeah, I know what you mean. I think you're right." He checked his watch. "Fuck, it's late. Are you ok getting home this late?" He looked concerned. It wasn't late at all compared to when I usually left work. He was so sweet to worry about me though.

"Don't worry about me, I live close to here."

"Oh really? How far? Like, a bus away?"

"Erm, no, closer actually. I normally get a bus home from the restaurant. I could probably walk back from here." I pointed towards the direction that the flat was. Georgina would probably be out again, so I planned to get a small tub of ice cream and chill out on my own.

"Fuck no, Fiona, you can't walk home alone in North London at this time of night. I'll walk you home." He already started walking before I could reply.

"Karl, are you sure? You don't have to. I'm honestly fine." I wanted him to though, of course.

He didn't even reply, instead we both just started walking towards the flat. As we walked along the dark streets of North London, the wind lashed at us, but we were wrapped up warm in our coats. I didn't have my scarf over my face so that I could talk to him. I looked up at the stars barely visible in the sky. Then I realised that it had started snowing. It was so romantic. The snowflakes landed on my face and made me shiver. It was beautiful. I couldn't help but smile to myself.

The weather was extremely uncomfortable. For many moons, Macha Land had been overwhelmed with heat. Spring had passed and Summer was upon them. And yet the Veil of Warmth was still cast over the island. Queen Fubuki had cast the Veil at the start of Winter to protect her people from falling shards of ice large enough to impale a horse. It melted the ice down to water and kept her people safe. However, that was no longer the case. Now, the Veil of Warmth dried up any rain that fell from the clouds.

The Southern Beach had become the Southern Desert, as it did every time the seasons changed, but this Summer it spread over more land than it ever had before. Sand villages were abandoned as the heat became unbearable. Any nature that once inhabited the desert was lost. Foliage caught fire and burned away. Grass turned to hay and mud turned to sand.

Closer to the capital in the Northern regions, the magickal creatures, villagers and other ethereal beings spent each day hunting for food, water and shelter from the sun. The merpeople swam to the bottom of the Lake where the sun and heat could not reach them. The markets were mostly empty, except for the tall, wooden stalls with sheets that draped down over them, providing the much needed shade for those who dared leave their homes.

Few did leave their homes. The Coven of Rosemary pooled their powers, tapping into the great energy of the planet and conjured as much food and water as they could. Those that could gather food and water, took it home and stayed there. Priests and priestesses in training made a small fortune by roaming around casting ice spells on those willing to pay for it.

Macha Land was in turmoil. It wasn't until a flaming bird appeared from the South that the fate of the realm began to change. People outside stared up at the ball of fire. It blazed like a comet. A pinkette of faeries in the markets pointed to the skies. Merpeople trusted their strong instinctive and psychic powers and swam to the surface to see it. Other creatures that were sitting around the Lake to cool by the water gazed up at her. She had returned.

The Phoenix cascaded down to the Veil and just as she reached it, a powerful burst of light and sound exploded all around her. The Veil of Warmth started to vibrate. Cracks began to form in it above various parts of the island, until it finally shattered into a myriad of white shards. They floated down on the realm. The heat that had been trapped rushed upwards. Great gusts – almost as strong as those of the Windy Planes – swept through the streets and the valleys. Across the realm, sounds of celebration filled the air as the people of Macha Land finally felt relief from the heat.

As Queen Fubuki descended from the sky, her blazing wings stretched out and a trail of smoke followed her tail. She felt the trapped heat escape past her into the sky. The clouds above her drifted away and all that remained was a clear blue sky. Her feet touched the ground outside her Palace of Crystal, but before she went to enter, she looked behind her at the vast landscape of Macha Land. It looked damaged and burned, but it would recover. Now that the Veil of Warmth had been withdrawn, all her land needed was time to heal itself.

* * *

Prince Hikaru, the Four Guardians and the rest of the crew safely sailed the ship to the Western dock in the Southern Desert. Queen Fubuki's spell on both the winds and the ship helped ensure their safe and speedy return to the Main Island. The crew on the upper deck were still damp from the water that had sprayed them. Prince Hikaru tried to coax Kaze down onto the sandy beaches but he was still frightened. The speed of the ship and the resulting vibrations in the lower deck stables had been constant and irritating. As they stepped onto dry land, they saw the Veil of Warmth being withdrawn. The Phoenix had returned to her realm. Even the horse watched peacefully as the white shards of light scattered into the skies, only to fade away and burn out. The shores of the Southern Desert were just beyond the Veil of Warmth, so they were able to see it dissipate right in front of them.

Endurance was the closest when it came down. A rush of air had swept past them as the heat trapped within the Veil escaped. The crew from the ship followed Prince Hikaru and the Four Guardians into the Southern Desert. The dock where they had left the ship was empty. The workers were gone. The closest village to them was Sandreach. That would be their first stop on the way to the capital.

The Four Guardians walked forward, following Endurance's lead. Strength quickly caught up with him and they walked side by side. Prince Hikaru was behind them all. He was concentrating so hard on his surroundings that he lost pace with the others. He couldn't see a single tree or any form of shrubbery in the close vicinity. The dock was dusty and silent.

They continued onwards into the mainland. Prince Hikaru remembered this place in the Summers that he had seen go by. It was always hot, but there was always life there. But now it was like all the energy was gone. It was now truly deserted. It struck Prince Hikaru just how similar the Southern Desert was to the second island. Having heard of the vile creatures that resided there under the control of the King of Truth, he started to fear the worst. He had to get to his Queen and tell her what had become of the South. They had to start preparing for battle.

Eventually the group made it to Sandreach. They heard the villagers talk frantically about the Veil being withdrawn, the winds that blew and the new, refreshing atmosphere around them. A centaur walked past Agility and gave him a hearty pat on the back that almost forced him to the floor. The town was rejoicing at the cooler air around them.

Prince Hikaru caught up with the others as they found the inn. He pulled out a crystal from his leather purse worth more than anything the innkeeper had ever seen and the innkeeper bowed to him at once.

"This way my Prince. We welcome you and your blessed beings here on this magickal night. I pray you sleep cool and deep," said the elderly, portly man as he bowed to them. Prince Hikaru turned to the group and opened his arms in welcoming.

"Let us rest on a soft bed and regain our energies. I will have food, ale and wine brought to your rooms shortly. We have seen many things. May your dreams bring you peace." The group continued to talk and laugh amongst themselves. They spent the night as friends under the same roof, drinking and forgetting the impending war.

* * *

The sky grew dark, but the stars shined brightly. The Main Stage glistened with pink and white gems. It was the first Songshow that Queen Fubuki had ever held at night. Regardless of the time, the entire realm was there. Not a single creature in her magickal world would want to miss this.

After a torturous season of heat and blisters, this was the tranquil haven they had been waiting for. Queen Fubuki organised the Songshow in order to bring joy to her people, after all the pain she had caused them. Despite it not being her fault, she couldn't help but feel guilty. Macha Land was still feeling the effects of what had been the hottest Summer in history.

In a cloud of fog she was teleported to the centre of the Main Stage. The crowd went quiet. The stars in the sky even appeared to be waiting for her.

"Kibou, Aijou, Jiyuu! Megami na no yo!" Her ancient words filled the air. They were slow, almost like she didn't sing them at all. Like the speech of faeries. A chant. "Megami na no yo..." she continued.

There was a group of Songmakers close to the outer edges of the Main Stage. They were there, waiting for her, ready. As she began the Songshow, they began to play. Violins, harps and pianos. Singers, dancers and performers. Melodies too complex for words to describe. Musical bubbles rose into the air and burst above the crowds. The music intensified and Queen Fubuki couldn't help but move her body.

The crowds cheered and stood up in excitement. Fireworks screamed into the sky. Music filled the air and people danced around. The night's sky covered everyone in a wave of ecstasy and peace. Before the Songshow Queen Fubuki had conjured ales and wines for those who sat close to the stage. Smiles and tears of joy were all she could see.

"Megami no megumi de, atashitachi ga ikiteiru no ne..." Her lyrics were mystic and ancient, filled with meaning beyond the comprehension of speakers of the common tongue. As the beat filled her, Queen Fubuki walked across the large crystal stage. She strutted along to the rhythm of the song, flicking her hair back and waving her hands in the air. The music took over her and she felt strong. She was the Goddess personified. Happy. Empowered. She was ready.

At the end of the chorus, the instrumental began and she broke into dance. Her dress fell away into waves of glitter and she threw her hands up. Pulsating to the song, she span around. Her legs kicked out and her arms stretched out around her. The crowd burst into roars of delight. As she walked along the stage that was transforming itself from a circular floor into a long walkway, she looked up. The stars were shining down on her. She was alive with energy. She blinked and a hundred small spheres of red lightning were spinning around her. They were like bees around a sweet pot of honey. With a final spin and a flick of her wrist, the spheres of lightning flew away into the audience and beautiful red powder rained down upon them. The song finished in a climax of drums and screams.

A night of wonderful music and dancing continued until dawn stirred in Macha Land. Queen Fubuki filled the hearts of her people with joy and happiness as she performed for them in the largest Songshow she had ever held. The Main Stage grew to five times its height and the fresh rays of sunshine sparkled through it. That marked the end of the Songshow and the fields of people cried with glee as she bowed to them.

"Farewell, my people," she said to screams of excitement.

Fubuki walked down from the Main Stage and covered herself in a red silk robe that she had crafted herself many moons ago. As the crowds began to disperse, she headed towards those amongst the crowd that were in no hurry to leave. They were the homeless and less fortunate of Macha Land.

She found a small child. Dirt on her cheeks and matted hair. The girl didn't notice the Queen approaching as she was facing the other way, but the shocked faces of those opposite her made her turn around. In a moment of awe, she bowed for the Queen. Her head was touching the floor and her hands were face down out in front of her. This was the most honourable way to kneel.

"Rise, my child. Did the Goddess bless you with a name?" Queen Fubuki asked, as she wiped clean her cheek with her right hand. Her red robe drifted down to the muddy floor. The child began to tear up and it became obvious that she could not speak.

"She has not been given the blessing of a name, nor a tongue, my Queen." A man said, slightly brazen from the wine. Fubuki sensed a pang of hostility from the stranger.

"I see. For that, I can only apologise on behalf of Her. The Goddess can be cruel, as well as kind. May I offer my blessings?" Queen Fubuki didn't take her eyes from the girl as she spoke. The girl's eyes began to water with disbelief. "And may you all rest tonight on full stomachs."

"My Queen, are your energies not better spent on our safety, not our woes? Should another attack happen..." The drunken man stopped as Queen Fubuki glanced at him. She gently let go of the girl and stood up straight. Her eyes were locked on the man.

"Presume not to know better than your Queen,
Worry not about what you have seen.
You know not of the struggles that I face,
And yet your fears I shall erase.
Take blessing in how I do not scold,
Your words are brave, but far too bold.
Her voice, I ask the Goddess permit,
A life of song will follow it.
Food and wine for your friends and kin,
Within this spell that I now spin."

She said the spell effortlessly and calmly. The small child gasped as if she has never truly taken in breath before.

Queen Fubuki's hands waved gently through the air in front of her and the air around them became heavy. From the earth around them, sprouted a variety of vegetables. A bolt of lightning came out of Fubuki's fingertips and landed close to them. Barrels of ale appeared after the smoke disappeared away into the sky.

Queen Fubuki was never one to be challenged, and yet she feared that the villager had a point. For all the ale she could conjure, it was nothing if she couldn't ensure her people's safety. She had to stop the King of Truth from taking her realm. She had to defend it. As she walked away to leave, the girl stood up, stuttering.

"A, a... k, kiss for the Queen." She managed. Her voice was dry and quiet. She was unsure of herself. As she finished her first sentence, she blew Queen Fubuki a gentle kiss. The air wafted towards Fubuki, filled with the scent of roses. The girl was a natural witch and Fubuki was even happier that she had given her a voice. Now she could cast her spells with ease.

"A kiss well received, my blessed child. A kiss well received."

* * *

The crew who had sailed the ship stayed in Sandreach for a few more nights, as they didn't have to hurry to their Queen like Prince Hikaru did. The payment that Prince Hikaru had left with the innkeeper was more than enough to keep them in wine, ale and food. Prince Hikaru didn't mind this. He knew that they had been through a lot. He bid them farewell. It was early sunrise when Prince Hikaru announced to them that he was ready to journey back to his Queen and most of the crew were still too drunk from the night before to even respond.

Strength and Endurance were in the same sleeping quarters. Defence and Agility were in their own personal ones. Prince Hikaru opened each of the three rooms to address them all at once.

"I bid you stay and rest. I must return to my Queen. She needs to know what the Southern Desert has become. We need to prepare for an attack. His army... made of dust and sand... is looming." Prince Hikaru held no emotion back, with his fists clenched and face twisted with fear. Endurance broke gently from Strength's embrace and walked to the doorway.

"We will all come with you, my Prince," he announced.

"Ay! We go with you. We will protect our Queen as well." Defence said as he grabbed his linens before standing.

"If you are to join me then we leave at once. I must go now. I am needed." Prince Hikaru did not intend to wait for them to rest their aching heads. He knew it was only their duty compelling them to join him. If they were truly needed by the Queen, she would have summoned them to her side already.

"My Prince. Go, we will only be slower as a group." Strength said finally.

Prince Hikaru nodded to them all and left for the door. Something inside him knew he had to get to her on his own all along. He did not have the magickal power to teleport to her and she hadn't summoned him either. It would also mean that he could observe the extent of the desertification as he travelled. He wanted to see for himself, so that he could report back to her. After the Southern Desert, he would travel through the Windy Planes and within a few nights reach the capital. With Kaze as his steed, it wouldn't take him long.

From the local markets of Sandreach, Prince Hikaru bought plenty of food and water. He had requested that his linens be washed by the innkeeper, but was told that they didn't have sufficient water.

The sun blazed down on them as they left Sandreach and headed North towards the capital. Kaze was a strong and loyal mount and would be able to gallop for most of the hours of daylight. It would be cooler at night, so they would rest in the next town, or somewhere that Hikaru could make a fire.

What Prince Hikaru didn't know was how vast the Southern Desert had become. They rode on together. Kaze kept good speed as the sand flicked out behind him. The hot rays of sun warmed Hikaru's skin and he could see it was already turning red. Droplets of sweat fell from his brow and tickled his neck. The journey continued on with nothing resembling another village in sight. Hikaru could only see sand and some scattered greenery.

Hikaru pulled out some fresh mint root from his satchel. Chewing it would supress his hunger. Slowing Kaze to a trot he scouted for water. Perhaps he would find a small oasis or spring, but there was nothing. He gave Kaze some of the water that he had bought from the market and soon they were off again.

"Good boy, go at your own pace until nightfall." As great a mount as Kaze was, he had ridden throughout the long and hot day. It would surely be time to stop for rest soon. Whilst focusing on nothing but reaching his Queen, Hikaru found his mind had begun to wander. His eyes drooped as he tired from having to constantly battle against the heat. His grip loosened and slowly he fell forwards into a light slumber.

Kaze continued to trot through the night. Whenever Kaze found water, he stopped and drank. Then he continued. Meanwhile, Hikaru slumbered peacefully on his mount's back and gained much needed rest.

They passed two smaller towns that were most probably abandoned. Hikaru woke suddenly as he began to lose his balance. Quickly grabbing the reins, he pulled himself steady.

"Kaze? Where are we? How long have we been riding for? Is it morning?" Hikaru ached all over. It hurt to even move. "Stop Kaze, we need water and food." Although as he said it, he realised that Kaze looked perfectly refreshed. Hikaru brought Kaze to a stop. They sat and rested together until their skin had cooled under the shade of two large woollen blankets held up with sticks. They must have been nearing the Windy

Planes by now. Yet, all Hikaru could see was more desert.

"Argh!" Prince Hikaru shouted out into the air. The realisation that he was trapped, alone in a dangerous place again had angered him. Next they would reach the Windy Planes and they would no doubt be even more desolate than here. "Fubuki!" He shouted for her. If only she summoned him, this would all be over. But his voice was not heard. It sounded out into the skies only to die away. He had to continue and make it to her as soon as he could.

For three more days they travelled. Their food and water reserves were gone, until they finally stumbled upon a small village where they found help. The elder of the village recognised him at once and ordered the villagers to put down their tools and come to the aid of their Prince.

"The sands are near to their end, my Prince. Another day's ride, and you will be done," said the Elder. He was too old to stand, but he bowed in his sitting pit. He then proceeded to refill the Prince's stocks.

"Thank you, wiseman, for your kindness. Your Queen will hear of it." Prince Hikaru said as he learned of his name.

The elder had spoken the truth. By nightfall they could see green land. Their time in the yellow void was ending. But this didn't please Hikaru greatly. The breeze had picked up. Trees rocked violently in the distance. Hikaru looked behind him as he rode slowly towards the green grass.

"This desert has surely taken over half of Macha Land." Hikaru noted. He had to report to his Queen.

There were no villages in the Windy Planes that Prince Hikaru knew about. No structure had proven strong enough to last. Trees and bushes grew around the edges, but none in the centre. Prince Hikaru would of course avoid the centre. It was a place of constant tornadoes and storms. He would travel along the right side. The Eastern shore of Macha Land was generally sheltered from the wind and full of towns and villages. The most famous housed the Coven of Rosemary. However, Hikaru had been travelling from the South Western dock and did not want to waste both his and Kaze's strength by travelling all the way to the other side of the Main Island. Instead, he would travel only as far East as he needed.

Hikaru spent hours fighting against the relentless winds. Kaze was heavy and able to hold his ground, but Hikaru wasn't. If, for a second, he let go of Kaze's reins he would have no doubt flown further into the eye of the Windy Planes, never to return. The winds would have sucked the air from his lungs and left him to fall against the hard ground.

They passed along the Eastern outskirts of the grey and gusty area. Tornadoes raged in the distance. All Hikaru could think about was getting back to his beloved wife. His Queen. Fubuki. She had to know about the Southern Desert. He had to see her again.

His linens clung to him on one side, whilst flapping loudly on the other. He squinted his eyes and let Kaze lead the way. He had no means of getting through on his own. Something in Hikaru knew that this was a test. The wind was so rough against him that it felt better to believe it was. He would be stronger after this. He would be more connected to everything. He had been lost within miles of woods. He had sunk deeper than any other in the cruel cold seas. He had walked for miles under the burning hot sun. Now he was fighting against these gale-force winds. These were his trials. This would make him strong enough for what was to come.

As he fought through the mind-numbing winds, both he and Kaze eventually made it to the other side. It took them two days. Midway they found a small hill that was fit for them to rest by, where they ate the supplies they had left. Kaze nibbled on whatever fresh grass he could find. When they finished the second day of walking, they could see the Main Stage in the distance. They completed the journey with Hikaru on his mount's back, riding away from the deadly planes and closer to the capital. The excessive heat had been gone for many days now and the markets would be bursting with treasures. Hikaru's mouth watered as he imagined the roasting meats and the fragrant wines that awaited him. Soon he would feast. Soon he would drink.

I remember walking to school one day in winter. I had a brown coat with a furry hood. It was extremely cold outside, but not quite snowing. Had it been snowing, school would have been cancelled. I would have been in a better mood if that had been the case. Instead, it was a usual school day. I was about 13 at the time. Life went on as normally as it could for someone like me. I had a good family, a couple of close female friends and didn't want for anything. In so many ways I was a lucky child. I didn't know any better.

Suddenly, my head was forced against the brick wall to my left. I felt the hard brick smash against my skull. Blood poured out and stained my uniform. One of the bullies had come up behind me whilst I was walking to school and had rammed me into the wall. Why did they keep doing this to me? He was alone. It wasn't like he even had anyone to impress. I walked to school an hour earlier than most kids to avoid getting bullied. Evidently, it wasn't always that easy.

My eyes closed themselves and pain took its hold on me. This wasn't fair. I tasted the blood. It was warm. I felt it on the back of my neck. It stank. I was used to it though. For what felt like a few seconds my eyes were closed and I was still on the floor. By the time I opened them again there were other children around me, some close up to me trying to talk. Others ignored me as they continued walking towards school. Judging by how many there were swarming the streets, it had to be close to the first bell by now. If I didn't get up soon I would be late. Perhaps I already was. My head ached. The brick wall to my left was red and dirty.

I had short hair then and a boy's school uniform on. I brushed my hair with my left hand lightly, and grimaced as it stung with pain. There was nothing I could do. He was one of the many boys that bullied me for being 'gay boy Eric'. All I could do was go to school, like any other day. If only it had been that simple.

The school bell rang as I came to the front gates. Various other students slowly walked in, but they didn't look the type to care about being late. They looked at me and laughed as I ran in, clutching my school bag. If you were late, you had to go via the student reception room and register. The punishment was usually detention if it was your first time. I could handle that. It just gave me more time to get my homework done, so I could enjoy my personal time at home. Fine.

I walked into the student reception area. The other late students all looked as if the world had done them an injustice. They formed a line so I joined the end. As I did, I felt another wave of pain from my head. The medical room wasn't far, so I decided to go there afterwards. There would be no point in telling them anything about the bully, but I could at least check that it wasn't too serious.

Before long the students in front of me had been seen and it was finally my turn. I pulled out my student book and opened it to the detention page.

"Reason for lateness?" The woman at the counter asked. She didn't even look at me. Her voice was bored and tired. A coffee was still steaming on her desk to her right.

"I smacked my head on a brick wall and was unconscious there for at least an hour." I said with a straight face. As I did, I noticed one of the boys that bullied me every day walked into the room. I had a feeling it was him. His eyes caught me standing there, with my hair stiff from the dried blood. His cocky grin was disgusting. What a dickhead.

"Sorry, you what?" She looked up at me in disbelief. She shook her head. "Don't lie to me."

"Miss, I'm not lying. Look. I was pushed by someone straight into the wall by the front gates." I turned my head and showed her, but she didn't want to see it. She didn't want to deal with what I was putting in front of her.

"That… that does look pretty bad, but don't lie to me about how it happened. I can tell when somebody has been in a fight, I'm not stupid. Hand me your student book and go to the medical room next."

"But no, I wasn't in a fight at all. Do I look like the kind of student that would fight anyone? I was attacked on the street."

"Don't lie to me. Student book. Now." Why wasn't she listening to me? If it had been an adult who had had their head smashed in, the police would have been involved. That wasn't the case for children. It was just classed as fighting.

"Fuck you then." The words fell out like vomit on her desk. All the children in the room started grinning and laughing. The bully was still there. His smirk was as wide as ever. The woman looked into my eyes and frowned. I knew why. She would have to take action, otherwise all the students would be swearing at her by the end of the day.

"Detention. Get out. Now!" She shouted. She stamped my otherwise untouched detention page with a dark red stamp. It had today's date and the words 'Level 5' on it. A 'Level 5' detention meant coming into school on a Saturday. It was the worst detention you could get without higher level teachers getting involved.

I stormed out in a fury. This was all so unfair. I had been the victim here. It was me who had had my head smashed into a brick wall and now I was the one getting detention. What the fuck? There was no justice. Nothing made sense. I was getting bullied for being gay, even though deep down, I knew that that wasn't even true. It was more complicated than that. I should have just been born a normal girl and none of this would be happening.

* * *

The detention on Saturday was abysmal. My parents were furious with me. They drove me in to make sure I got there on time. I hadn't told them the details of how I got it, or what really happened on that day. It wouldn't have changed anything. It would have only made things worse. More people would have got involved and it would have stayed with me for days. This way, I would just go to the detention for swearing at a teacher, and be done with it. It was the more mature thing to do.

Wearing my uniform felt very stupid. Saturday was the day I washed my uniform. Now that would have to be tomorrow. It messed everything up. I was only thirteen. This was all so unfair. I walked up to the main hall. The teacher's car park was empty except for the headmaster's car. Some people joked that he lived at school because he was always there. But I figured that if he drove in then how could he live at school? Wasn't that obvious?

I was the third student to arrive for Saturday detention. I sat myself down at the desk nearest to the window. I planned to read my book after finishing the essay. The essay was our 'punishment'. We had to write about how sorry we were for whatever we did. The headmaster would then read it before we went home. If it wasn't sincere enough, usually you would have to re-write it. At least that's what the other kids in my class told me. Ironically, I had gained a small amount of street-cred once word got out that I'd been given a Level 5.

The rest of the students came in. There were about twenty of us in total. I was in the top twenty badly behaved students for this week. I felt so ashamed. I swore however provoked I got, I would never do that again.

"You, boy, why are you here? You're a new face." The headmaster pointed to me and I stood up.

"I swore at a teacher, sir." I said calmly. Some of the other students laughed at my camp voice.

"I see. That is very disrespectful. Give me six A4 pages as to why that is wrong." He moved on to the next student. It felt like he went easier on the students that he recognised.

"Rebecca... again? How many times have I told you? You can't go around wearing your skirt so short. You will keep getting dragged here every Saturday until you stop. Is that what you want, Rebecca?" His tone was soft and understanding. Looking back, it was also very patronising, but Rebecca didn't seem to notice that.

"Sorry, sir. Won't do it again, sir." She lied. She sat down and pulled out her phone.

Within 30 minutes I had finished three sides of writing. The others looked at me as if I was an alien. We would be here for five hours, why was I rushing? I didn't care. Fuck them all. Fuck everything. Nothing was fair. Nothing mattered. In my essay I wrote everything that had happened. From the walk into school when I was attacked, to the teacher ignoring it in reception. I had decided that this was all too unfair. I demanded justice.

After I finished writing, I pulled out my book. Some of the other kids laughed, almost in disbelief. I could feel the headmaster watching me too, but I didn't care. Soon he would know my story, and soon something would be done about it. I read my book peacefully for the rest of detention. Before I knew it, it was time to give in my essay and head home. My parents said I could walk home and if people laughed at me in my uniform then so be it.

Rebecca handed in her essay, so I followed quickly behind her. Then another student followed behind me. The headmaster read her essay through quickly and nodded. She left through the doors and headed home. Her headphones went straight in her ears and a lighter was ready in her hand. Then it was my turn. I handed it over, and waited for his reaction.

"Very good. You can go."

"What? Did you not read it, sir?" I said. I was careful not to get myself in more trouble by sounding rude.

"Just get out, before I give you another detention." He said. His eyes had barely glanced over the paper. Before I had a chance to get angry, the boy behind me had given in his essay. I was pushed aside and made my way begrudgingly to the door. I had never felt like this before. I was so frustrated. So alone. So angry. It felt like everyone was against me. As if I was alone in a fantasy world where everyone was my enemy.

"Hey, you ok?" A voice came from behind me. I had found a bench outside and was sitting in disbelief. I looked round and it was the boy who was behind me in the queue to leave detention. I knew who he was, I had seen him before. He was very handsome and had a sense of apathy about him that was very cool. He was in the higher level classes though, so there must have been something going on in his brain.

"No, I'm fucking pissed off to be honest. This is bullshit." I let it out.

"Calm down mate, don't let it get to you. What did you do?" He smiled at me as he spoke. He gently nudged my shoulder with his fist as he tried to cheer me up. His eyes were dark. He had a rucksack on that was grey with badges on the side. He wore black vans instead of school shoes and had chipped black nail varnish on. He was beautiful.

"I swore at a teacher. That's all, I know. It's just... not like me. I shouldn't be here." I was still angry, even though I was enjoying talking to him.

"I'm Karl by the way." He introduced himself. "Just forget about it all for today, ok?"

"I'm Eric. Thanks. I guess I really shouldn't let it get me down." I let out a sigh and stared out into the empty school car park.

"Exactly. You looked pretty content reading your book anyway." He laughed and pointed at the book still in my hand. I laughed back. It was true. It could have been worse. "What way are you going? Fancy getting some chips?" It was only the cool kids that got chips from the chip shop by the station on the way home from school. Then I realised it was Saturday and I could technically do whatever I wanted. If it meant spending more time with Karl then I was happy.

That was the day I met Karl Stevenson. He changed my outlook on life as a teenager with no effort at all. We didn't know it then, but we would eventually get caught up in a complex web of emotions, drama and pain. I would fall madly in love with him. He would fall in love with the girl inside me, who I should always have been. The world would think we were a gay couple, but no one knew the truth. We experimented together. Partied together. Drank together. And at the heart of it, Karl and I became the closest of friends. We went on holiday together. I stayed round his house. No matter what anyone else said, we *were* in love. We were happy. He made me happy. He made me feel like a girl. Although it was never that easy, and it tortured us both every day because society wasn't ready. He wasn't ready to love me. I wasn't ready to be loved.

"Fighters! Now we march. We march to protect our realm. Fight for your Queen! Fight for your homes! Fight for your freedom!"

Prince Hikaru's voice bellowed out. Hundreds of soldiers stood proudly before him. Humans, centaurs, sprites, pixies and elves. Tall and small, yet each and every one powerful. The entire realm rallied to her side. A field of weapons glistened in the light from above. Since the day the innocent had been killed by the King of Truth, her people had prepared to fight for her. She told them of the battle on the Volcano Island. Her Songshow had served to bring comfort to her people, but also to warn them. To rally them. To give them the strength they would need.

Prince Hikaru would lead the army. He had the trust of the people and the necessary military knowledge. As he prepared for the march South, he stood facing the many creatures before him. His armour was magicked to be stronger than ever and a bright red colour. Her colour. The colour of passion, fire and love. Gloves and wristbands shielded his hands. His linen armour was wrapped tightly around his chiselled muscles. He wore red linen breeches, with silver embroidery down the side. The light danced off it. His weapon of choice was his longest Katana. The sheath was as dark as night. It had no hand guard, but instead was just curved and black. On one side, there was a silver Phoenix carved into the handle.

"Forward!" He bellowed with his right arm high in the air, holding his deadly sword. The army before him echoed with a flood of battle cries. Their feet began to move in unison and the herd of creatures moved as one. They would head South to meet the King of Truth's army on the battlefield.

This was exactly how the Coven of Rosemary had foreseen it in their visions. Not a moon after Queen Fubuki's return, they had approached her. They had seen him and his army of terrifying beasts. Queen Fubuki and Prince Hikaru were in the Palace planning their attack, when they had reached her.

"My Queen, we have come to warn you." The eldest of them had said. Her hair was white and long. Her eyes were like pearls, lost amongst the wrinkles of her face.

"I know he has an army. I have felt it. I have seen it. What else can you see, High Priestess?" She was eager to gain the upper hand. Here in her Palace of Crystal she felt powerful. It was her home, her safe haven. If only she could battle the King of Truth here.

"He comes from the South. He comes with a thousand creatures made of sand, metal and dust. They are ravenous and inhumane. You will have no choice but to fight. The battle will be perilous. Many will perish." The elder spoke as her eyes turned black. She was recalling her visions. The surrounding witches closed their eyes and nodded. It was a mystical moment.

"The South?" It dawned on Queen Fubuki. "It must be the land. He is at his most powerful in the desert. But Autumn winds blow of late. Surely the Southern Desert retreats."

"This season has been different. The Veil of Warmth kept the heat locked in. This Autumn will come too late. He will be upon us." The elder came back into herself and her eyes returned to normal.

"I see. Thank you, High Priestess. I will have Prince Hikaru gather an army and march down to meet him. We will fight the King of Truth South of the Lake. If we march into the desert, we are his. Instead we will wait in the heart of Macha Land." Queen Fubuki explained her plans. Prince Hikaru stood up next to her to listen closely.

"My Queen, you mean we would allow our Southern towns be destroyed? Why should we not meet him at the shores?" Prince Hikaru argued.

"With the Windy Planes to the West, and the Sea to the East, his army will have no choice but to attack us face on in the land where we are strongest. Then we will slaughter his army of dust." Her plan was straightforward. Her voice was thick with power.

"He will not fall for that. He surely knows this land, which he claims for himself. You saw him atop the Ice Mountain, he will know not to fight you there." Prince Hikaru made a valid point. The witches nodded. "What of this? We march further South to meet him and fake a retreat. He will follow us if he believes the advantage is his. He will then be fighting between the Windy Planes and the sea. A fine way to stop fire and stone." Queen Fubuki and Prince Hikaru looked at each other in agreement.

"Yes. So it shall be done. Prince Hikaru, go. Form the biggest army Macha Land has ever seen. May Macha of the Morrigon herself watch over you. Goddess be with you." With that Queen Fubuki leant in and kissed her beloved. He reached his hand around her and pulled her in. It could have been their last kiss. He would ensure that the universe felt their love one last time.

"What of the Coven of Rosemary?" The elder asked her Queen. "What will you have us do?"

"I entrust you with the most serious of tasks. I must fulfil my own destiny. However, the destiny of the realm will go whichever way the universe wills it. It is in your hands, should I leave this world. Pray you go back to the Tower of Magi. Cast your strongest spell for protection. Meditate. Chant. Use your magicks and cleanse this island of whatever evil breaks our defences. It is your collective power that will be the last in our defence again the King of Truth." Queen Fubuki knew she might fall. She knew that he was strong, even if she had grown stronger in the past moons. She had to leave something in place in case the battle ended with her life being lost forever.

"So it shall be done, my Queen. Let it be set in stone." The elder spoke in a powerful, chanting voice.

"Let it be set in stone." Queen Fubuki repeated. She gestured them to leave and make their preparations.

As the greatest army in Macha history strode through the channel between the Windy Planes and the Eastern edge of the biggest island in Macha Land, Queen Fubuki remained in her Palace. Of course she would not abstain from the fight. Far from it. She would be the key to its victory. This was what she had hoped and prayed for. She closed her eyes and felt her beloved lead her people to fight for her. She was meditating in her Palace and felt connected to everything.

When she woke from her meditation, she slowly began to walk outside her Palace. She was completely skyclad. With her right hand, she drew a circle in the air in front of her and a white spherical ball of light surrounded her.

"I summon my Four Guardians. Strength, Endurance, Defence and Agility. Be here and protect your Queen. I summon you!" She called out into the circle. Four blue flames lit up around her and with them came her protectors. They knelt instantly before her and without any words took their positions in the circle. She was performing her final summoning spells.

"My mount, my noble pathtaker. Kaze. I summon you!" In a flash of lightning her precious horse was by her side. He leapt up in the air and rode around the inner perimeter of the large white sphere that they were inside.

"I summon my swords! I summon my staff!" She shouted into the air, and suddenly from the clouds above they came spinning down. Her staff landed with a thud in her hand and her three swords flew to their place behind her back. They were attached to her, ready to be drawn.

"Earth, Air, Fire, Water,
Lead the lamb into slaughter,
Air, Fire, Water, Earth,
The Phoenix rises to rebirth,
Fire, Water, Earth, Air,
Save my realm from its despair,
Water, Earth, Air, Fire,
I cast this spell and raise it higher!"

Kaze reared as the energy around them grew to a climax. The Four Guardians held their positions as she spoke. Red lightning pulsed from the tip of her pentacle staff and with it she span widdershins. The energy within the circle exploded and the spherical ball of light burst all around them. Brilliant white light scattered out and filled the air. It was so bright that they had to shield their eyes at first. Strength was the first to lay eyes upon her when the lights went out. She was beauty personified.

Covering her curvy and lustrous body was a gown of pure white. It was a softer fabric than any that had ever touched her skin. The top split into two cuts of fabric that crossed behind her neck. Under her breasts, the dress was wound tightly around her waist and orbited around her hips and thighs. It burst out in a cascade of material. Layers of silk and netting were draped over the white gown. Her legs were bare underneath. Her feet touched the ground. She connected to the earth below her. She was connected to the Goddess.

In her hair, she wore seven large silver needles. Each kept her hair in place. Not a strand was loose, other than her fringe, which framed her face. The seven needles were connected with bells, golden chains, feathers and metal encased crystals. Four needles for her Guardians. One for her horse. Another for her beloved. Then finally one for the Goddess who watched over her. Fubuki's lips were red. Her eyes black. Around her neck, fingers and wrists she wore crystals wrapped in silver chains. Red rubies and purple amethysts. They sparkled as she moved.

Her hands were covered in sleeves that started halfway down her arms, fastened by red ribbons that weaved in and out of the main fabric. The sleeves were decorated with delicate patterns that looked like great flames weaving in and out of her. She looked like Venus. Like Hecate. Like Macha. She was the Phoenix. She was the Queen. The Goddess herself.

"It is time. Prepare yourselves." She said. With that, she raised her staff once more and called a different circle. This one was to break the rules of time and space. In a flash of energy, the entire area around her and her protectors changed. She had teleported them all to where Prince Hikaru was currently leading the army. They appeared before him in a burst of red light. The army of the realm roared with courage and power.

"My Queen, you are here." He sounded pleased, with a hint of fear for her.

"My love. I am here to give you this gift. The Four Guardians will fight together with you. My horse will carry you once again." She spoke loudly, so that the Four Guardians heard too.

"What? My Queen? We must stay by your side, and yours alone." Defence shouted back.

"He is right, we will protect you." Strength added. Endurance and Agility were equally bewildered.

"This is what I demand. You will protect your Prince. He may become your King before the night ends."

"No! Fubuki! Don't you dare say that!" Hikaru screamed. Even he was shocked at his own outburst. The Guardians watched on silently. He couldn't speak to her like that here, not at a time like this. Even if it was out of love.

"Prince Hikaru. March my army onwards and fight. Protect my people at all costs. Meanwhile, I have my own quest to face. I have my own path to follow. There will be no words of rebuttal." She said calmly. She had rehearsed this small and simple speech for many nights before this day. "Go forth, Hikaru. Please" she added quietly just to him. Hikaru nodded.

With her staff still in hand and her white dress flowing out around her, she walked towards the Southern Desert. Fire began to burn where her feet met the ground and it caught her dress. The fabric didn't burn away. Instead it sparkled like embers. Soon she was fully ablaze, but she kept walking. Her army behind her did the same. Prince Hikaru and the Four Guardians walked forwards. It was not how they had envisioned the battle would begin, but it would no doubt end in the same way.

"They are here, I can sense them." Queen Fubuki said out loud. She didn't know if anyone even heard her. The fires took her and great blazing wings grew from her sides. Her dress seemed to manipulate the flames and make them stronger. She was a great white faery of fire. The red surrounded her and she flew up into the sky. She was not quite the Phoenix, nor was she human. She was a fusion. A combination. The mix of a beautiful Queen and a bird made of fire. She flapped her blazing wings and flew further into the sky.

The air around her was pure. The ground below her was yellow and vast. She could see it all from here, high above the centre of Macha Land. In the distance, where there was only sea, she could see heavy grey clouds forming. Storms were brewing on the edge of the world. Powers were being raised on either side that the realm had never witnessed before. Ominous shades of purple and grey filled the skies, but the storms seemed too far away to influence the battle that was moments away from her. Now was her time. Now was the hour. She had her army. She had the power.

Getting ready everyday was painfully frustrating. If it was too hot in my house my makeup wouldn't stay on and I didn't know how to stop it from running. Georgina said she didn't know how either, as she was always cold. She looked at me with a sad, sympathetic face as I frantically ran around my room. I was going to be late for work again if I didn't sort myself out. It was like this every morning. Without makeup I was... not myself.

"At least you work at a restaurant, so your hours are better." Georgina said, trying to help.

"What do you mean?" I didn't look at her as I spoke. I didn't have time. I had to do my eye makeup, then at least I could finish the rest on the bus. That was not always the best idea though – I would get stared at even more.

"Well, you're not up and out at 7 a.m., are you? You work from around 10 a.m., so you have the morning to get ready every day."

"Yeah, I guess so. It literally takes me all morning though. Think about it. You don't have to shave your face every day, do you?" I was getting annoyed and defensive. I had time for blusher next if I was quick.

"No. I don't. But men do?" I couldn't tell if she was now trying to piss me off or not.

"Men don't shave as closely as I have to. I shave once down and then back up again, otherwise I have stubble by the end of my shift. Can you imagine how dangerous that is coming back on the bus home at night?" I was getting louder and suddenly felt bad. Maybe she was just trying to help.

"Fine. Sorry Fiona. Calm down, I was just saying." She looked down at the floor and went to leave.

"No, I'm sorry. I'm just stressed and I hate being late. I have to go, but have a nice Saturday, and see you tonight. Shall I bring dinner home? My treat."

"That would be lovely." She smiled and went back to watching TV. Before long, I was on the bus and was semi-satisfied with my makeup. It was the best it could be for now. I had contoured my nose to look thinner and my cheekbones to look higher. My eyes were my most feminine feature, so I focused on those to draw attention away from my chin and jaw. I hated my chin and jaw. They were so manly and disgusting.

My hair was growing, but it wasn't long enough to hide my face entirely. Recently I had been scrunching it up with mousse, which looked nicer. When it was straight, my face looked longer and my manly brow was more visible. When I curled it, it made my face appear rounder and with a fringe I could cover my brow. I just had to make sure I still showed my eyes.

It was lucky that I had been promoted at the restaurant, otherwise I would have had to have my hair in a bun or ponytail everyday like the other women. Paul had spoken to the owner and they agreed to make me a supervisor. My pay went up considerably and I still got to keep my tips. I was so proud when Paul told me.

"Well, the owner didn't mind. You practically do a supervisor's role at the moment anyway. It's just about me sorting out the paperwork." Paul grinned. He hated paperwork and everyone knew it. He moaned about it almost every day. "Just try to not be late, ok?"

"Thank you so much Paul. I promise I won't be! Working here is... it's just amazing. You are the most understanding boss I have ever had." My only other boss was Marie, so that wasn't hard, but it still felt nice to say.

I could see the restaurant from the bus window. Karl and I had been texting each other since we went for drinks. I had time on the bus to reply to his latest message quickly. It always made me smile when I thought of him. He always rang me in the evening to make sure I was home safe.

Only a few people had looked at me on the journey, so my makeup must have been ok after all. I checked my mirror one last time. I looked fine, so I grabbed my bag and was ready to get off the bus.

My mind wandered to my dreams. I still had them every night. The Queen, all powerful, living in a mystical land. I wished I was like her and could do whatever I wanted. She was so amazing. So strong. All I wanted was to be strong. A strong, independent woman.

I still had a long way to go though. I still cried every time I changed my hormone patch. Georgina called them 'Emotional Wednesdays' and 'Sullen Sundays'. I would put my new patch on in the morning and anything could set me off. A penguin documentary. An old song on the radio. Within seconds, I would be blubbering.

The restaurant was still closed, so I went in through the back door. The room was filled with the sound of the float being emptied out into the till. Paul was in, but no one else was around yet. Despite all my panicking, I had actually made it to work on time. It was still very dark and stuffy as the windows hadn't been opened yet. I flicked on a couple of the lights as I walked in. Paul looked up from the till.

"Fiona, morning. You alright?" He said, still sounding half asleep.

"Hey Paul, I'm good!" I shouted back to him as I headed to the staff room to try to check my makeup with the time I had left. My eyeliner could always use a going over. My hair would need tweaking. Anything I could do to look more feminine. Anything to stop the customers staring at me and making comments.

"Oh, by the way," Paul said. "I may need to leave early tonight. Are you ok cashing up? It's gonna be pretty late tonight, I imagine. Is that ok?"

He stopped what he was doing and looked at me to see my reaction.

"Yeah, of course. No problem. Alysha is doing a double shift today too right?"

"Think so. She'll probably stay with you. Keep her away from the drink, ok? You can both have a glass once you're finished, but not before." Paul offered kindly. I smiled and nodded.

"Sure, thanks Paul," I added before I headed downstairs. I lit up the rooms one by one as I got to each of them. The owner was sometimes in on a Saturday, but not today. He didn't come in much at all anymore, come to think of it. Paul said he was getting fairly ill. He was an old Italian guy, who was divorced from his wife and had nothing to live for other than this restaurant. He kind of freaked me out a bit, so as sad as his situation was, I was glad he didn't come in much.

To be honest, I was scared to stay late. But I had to. It was my job, I was a supervisor now. The money made it worth it, but it wasn't just about the money. I was finally part of something. I had responsibilities. I was accepted. I was the supervisor of a restaurant in London. Fine, it wasn't anything like the office job I had before, but still. I enjoyed it and for now that was all that mattered to me.

Before I knew it, the rest of the staff had arrived and it was time to start working on the restaurant floor. I didn't get a section of tables anymore, instead I would float around and keep an eye on things. I saw it more like problem solving. If a particular area needed help, I would go there. I would help clear tables, give tips to new staff, or check the customers were happy. Sure, sometimes I got some funny looks. I was very tall, my hair was still not very long and it was obvious that I was transgender. One day, I would pass completely as a woman and the looks would stop. That's all I could think to myself to keep going. Imagining that this was it, forever, would be soul-crushing. Imagining being in my thirties and still not passing as a woman would be too depressing.

I didn't have to stick to the black uniform anymore either, but I had to look smart. I wore a white blouse under a long black top that went down to my knees. I only ever wore clothes that covered everything. The cuffs and the collar of the shirt were visible and brought a bit of light to the otherwise dark outfit. Even though it was a shirt, it was clearly a girl's shirt, so I was happy with how feminine I looked.

Our team of ten worked hard throughout the day. Alysha was practically running the whole second floor. When it was busy, I sometimes saw Paul coming up from the office and helping out too. Ellie and a couple of other newer staff members kept stopping for small two minute breaks in the kitchen, but that was understandable.

Alex had only been working here for a week or so. He had been rude to me from the moment he saw me. When he found out I was a supervisor, he openly expressed his surprise. The words 'someone like her' were uttered. He was lucky that Paul wasn't there to hear him, otherwise he would have probably been fired on the spot. Or worse, had Alysha been there... Who knows what she would have done. I tried to not let it get to me. He was entitled to his opinion, as bigoted as it may have been.

I walked into the kitchen to find Alex and a couple of the male chefs laughing. They turned around to see me and the laughter stopped immediately. It was replaced with childish grins and smirks. It felt like I was in secondary school again. I shoved the plates in the sink.

"Alright there mate?" Alex called out to me, feigning sincere concern.

"I'm not your mate. Can you get to your section please?" I didn't need to be nice. I would keep things strictly professional. Perhaps I sounded bitchy, but I didn't care. Alex opened his mouth to speak, but before he could reply, Paul walked by quickly with dirty plates. He walked straight back out and I followed him.

The rest of the shift went by normally, until I found a pleasant surprise waiting for me at the bar. It was Karl. He was there again, just like before. Drinking a beer and playing on his phone. I made my way there and started tidying around the bar area.

"Hey Karl, what brings you here?" I said. I was standing opposite him before he even noticed I was there. He looked up from his phone.

"Fiona! There you are." A smile spread across his face and his eyes widened. He was so cute when he smiled.

"You ok? What's up?"

"Oh, nothing. I'm good. Actually, I came to speak to you." He suddenly looked nervous.

"Me? Why?" I started to remember how close we were before everything that I had gone through.

"Fiona, I was wondering... Are you seeing anyone at the moment?" He looked at me, shyly.

"What? No, of course not. What makes you ask that?" My heart was racing. I couldn't help but smile. What had just happened? Was he asking me out? No way.

"Well, I would have thought that was obvious. Look, I really enjoyed the other night and if you wanted to, I'd like to do it again sometime. What do you think?" He let himself relax and his natural confidence came through. When he smiled at me, I felt my legs weaken. Old feelings came rushing back.

"But, Karl, it's complicated. I'm..." I couldn't bring myself to say it. Not only was I embarrassed, but I was also ashamed. If I had been any other girl, I could just have said yes. I could just have dated him and seen where it went. The first guy I ever loved was asking me out. Of course I wanted to say yes. But how could I? Me? Now? Guys that were interested in me were only looking for a 'girl like me'. They wanted the exact part of me that I hated the most. And, if a guy somehow couldn't tell, I wouldn't be able to date them because I wasn't ready yet. I wasn't... finished yet. They would run a mile if they knew.

"I know. I know you're trans, Fiona. It's just a date though. For old time's sake, as they say." Karl said calmly. So was he interested in *that?* I hoped not.

Although he did have a point. He had only asked me out for drinks. Maybe I was overthinking things. I did do that a lot.

"Ok, well, it would be nice to catch up some more. Sure, why not." I nodded and smiled. The idiotic chef assistant Alex caught my eye as he was going to leave the restaurant. He walked behind Karl and looked straight at me.

"Great, that's great. Are you free tonight?" Karl began, but before I had time to say no, the chef assistant mumbled something.

"See you tomorrow tranny." My face dropped. It all happened so fast. Karl span around and in moments had the guy against the wall with his arm pressing forcefully against his neck. I threw the cloth I was holding down onto the counter and ran out from behind the bar. Paul and some other members of the team were already running towards us.

"Karl, no, it's fine. Get off, it's fine!" I shouted. I could feel everyone's eyes on me. I didn't want this. I went bright red and wanted to disappear.

"You heard what he said." He shouted and then looked at him. "Apologise!"

"I'm sorry! Fuck. Get off me." He clearly didn't expect that. Karl loosened his grip and Alex ran off. Paul looked at me in horror. The entire restaurant was staring at us.

"Paul, I'm sorry. He's with me. I'm so sorry." I said with my head down.

"Fiona, why are you apologising? That guy just insulted her, he should be fired." I felt like Karl was making it worse.

"He what? Alex? No way, he's not like that." Paul was shocked.

The idiot didn't get fired, but he got a written warning. Since then, Alex and the rest of them showed me a lot more respect too. The scene that Karl caused was extremely embarrassing, but a part of me was also glad it happened. Karl didn't need to defend me like he had. It made me feel safe, like I could trust him. When we were younger, he always protected me from the bullies, so I guess some things never change.

Paul let me go on my break early, so Karl and I went for a walk. He needed a moment to cool down as well. We found a small coffee shop and I picked a muffin and ordered a mocha. Karl got a latte. Karl told me to go and get a seat. I tried to give him some cash, but he wouldn't take it. As I walked into the stylishly decorated room, I found myself smiling.

The smell of coffee beans and the gentle chatter of the surrounding tables filled the air. I didn't focus on any of the people here like I normally did. It was all just noise, anyway. Even looking at them was just like looking at a painting in a gallery. It didn't matter if they were staring at me. I was with Karl. My eyes, my mind and my body were focused on him. He stood there, confident, charming and masculine. He had evolved from a rebellious teenager into a mature man. But even during his delinquent times, he still made me feel safe. Always safe. That brought about a different kind of masculinity in him that I loved dearly. I realised that now, all these years later. Whilst I was failing to try to be a boy, he did it so naturally. He was meant to be a boy. I wasn't. I was never a gay guy. I was never truly attracted to gay guys. I was a woman and I only found myself attracted to straight men. But back then relationships with gay guys were the closest I could get to finding love. It all made a lot more sense now.

He glanced my way and our eyes met for a moment. I looked down shyly at the floor and held back a smile. Soon, he was sitting opposite me and we were talking about what had happened earlier in the restaurant. Then we organised our next date and talked about old school friends and the music we used to listen to. It made me want to spend the whole day sitting in bed listening to it all again.

"Do you remember Devon?" He asked me. How could I not?

"Of course. I'll never forget that."

I saw it in my head like re-watching my favourite film as we spoke. Old feelings and old memories. But with old memories, came old pain. I was a new person now. I wasn't Eric anymore. It felt important for me to remind myself that.

"I'd love to go again, as the new me. As a woman. A part of me wants to relive all of the best memories of my life."

"One of the best memories of your life? Eric, that's so sweet." He looked at me. Then he realised. I looked down and faked a smile to stop him from seeing how much it hurt me. "Oh fuck, I'm so sorry. Fiona. Shit, I didn't mean to upset you, it's just old habits die hard."

"I know. Don't worry hun, it happens." I put on a brave face, but it did hurt.

"Seriously, I mean it. Fiona, you know I understand you. I understand you better than most. To me, you were always a girl. It was just your name. It's hard to explain..." He grabbed my hands from the table and held them in his. "Look at me. Do you trust me? I won't hurt you."

Where did that come from? Suddenly everything was getting so serious. My mind was a mess, my heart was beating fast and my stomach was filled with butterflies. I nodded and smiled, genuinely this time.

He smiled too, but I could feel a sense of sadness or even pity in his face as well. I could tell that something important was about to begin.

There was always a party on Friday after college. Someone in our group would have a house party, even if it was last minute. Our group was happier than usual finishing school that day as we had a week off for half-term. The school car park filled with kids, ranging from young children to young adults, as it hit 3 p.m. I could see them all leaving from the library windows. It looked warm and the blue skies made everyone smile just that little bit more.

I noticed Georgina leaving with that French guy Stéphane through the main school exit. They had been seeing each other for about two months now. He was totally wrong for her. I always thought she should have chosen Ali. He had been in love with Georgina since Year 7, but she never noticed. Or she never wanted to. Either way, she was holding hands with Stéphane. We had planned to meet at the party later.

The business report I was writing wasn't due for a couple of weeks, but as I was halfway through it, I thought it would be easier just to finish it tonight. That way I could really enjoy tonight and my holiday next week. Karl and I were going down to Devon for the week. Karl's mum had rung mine. It was all sorted. Our friends laughed and said it was our honeymoon, so where was the wedding? They made their jokes, but we didn't care. We were best friends and we wanted to have a break from school.

Karl had just passed his driving test, so he was excited to drive his new car for a long distance for the first time. I loved sitting in the passenger's seat and listening to music on a long drive, so that suited me just fine. We had booked a cottage, with separate rooms. It wasn't huge, but we didn't need it to be.

I pulled my mind back to my business report. The cash flow forecast didn't match up to the business' five-year plan. That was a point to raise in the essay. The library was filled with the sound of pencils scratching away at paper. Another hour should do it.

Later that evening I dropped my school stuff at home. It didn't take me long to get ready. I played with my hair, changed my shirt and that was it. I had bathed the night before, so I didn't need to do anything else. Getting ready as a boy was so much easier than as a girl.

I practiced my smile in the mirror and walked out the door. The bus stop was only a few steps away. The air was cooler and it was starting to get dark. I had barely anything to carry with me and yet I always carried a bag. It was a brown shoulder bag, with a small zip-up pocket on the front that I kept my phone and wallet in. My friends said I looked stupid with a bag all the time, but I didn't care. It made me feel better, even if it was virtually empty.

Georgina was at the party already. She was mixing cocktails in the small kitchen that opened out onto the garden. The others would be here soon. They were from a different friendship group to Karl and the other girls. They all knew of each other, mostly through me, but they didn't hang out together.

I grabbed a drink and took a long gulp. It had been a long week of assignments and deadlines.

"So Lee is coming tonight, you know?" Georgina teased. Lee was the British-born Chinese guy who had wanted to get with me for ages now. I probably would give in eventually.

"Oh really and why does that bring such a big smile to your face?" I said, feigning a naïve tone.

"No reason, no reason. I just love seeing two people close to me getting even closer." She said slyly.

"He is kind of cute I guess, he always holds the door open for me at college." We laughed together. I did feel nervous at the idea of him being here tonight and imagined what would happen. Would we kiss? Would I like it? Everyone knew we were both gay, so I doubt anyone would be surprised. None of the dangerous crowd would be here tonight, as it was Georgina's friend's party. Maybe I could let myself enjoy the moment.

The music started playing and the other guests flooded in. Georgina was busy with Stéphane in the garden. A friend of Lizzy's was talking to me in the kitchen, but I wasn't really focused on the conversation. I was looking out for Lee. I had drunk three of Georgina's cocktails already. I was probably being more obvious about looking for him than I should have been.

People were walking through the garden gate outside the house. I could see from the kitchen window, but not very clearly. I could tell it was him though, with three other girls I had seen around school. Georgina jumped down from Stéphane's lap and dragged them all into the kitchen to sort out drinks. Our eyes met and I looked down shyly. He grinned and came straight over to me. The sound of blended ice filled the room. He put his arm against the wall to my right.

"Hey, glad to see you here, cutie." He whispered in my ear. I went red and felt my heart begin to beat faster.

"Hey, nice to see you too. Want a drink?" I tried to claw back some confidence to not look too pathetic, but I could tell that he liked how shy I was. He found it cute. I liked being thought of as cute. It was the closest thing I could get to being thought of as feminine. But that confused me. He liked me because I was a cute boy, not a cute girl. It was all so confusing, but I didn't let myself think about it now. I dared not speak a word of what was running through my mind. I grabbed us some drinks. I drank. I just drank.

More people flooded in and the front room became the dancing room. Music, heavy with bass, echoed throughout the house and out into the street. Faces I had seen before, and those I hadn't, mixed together like the different drinks in my stomach. The music took over until I didn't care what I looked like. I kept drinking and dancing. Georgina joined me for songs she liked, then went to smoke outside for ones she didn't.

Lee was with me the whole time. We danced together. We danced on each other. His hands were on my hips as if he owned me. Some of the other guys laughed and made jokes, but I was too drunk to care. Lee was too mature to care. I see now how desperate I was just to be loved. His hands stayed there. It made me feel safe. Sexy. Wanted.

"We should see if there is a spare bedroom" he shouted in my ear. If the music hadn't been so loud that I could barely hear him, it could have been extremely embarrassing. Luckily, even with him shouting, I could only work out what he was saying because of his eyes. They screamed louder than anything else.

I didn't want him in that way. He was cute, but not my type. What I did want more than anything was to be wanted though. That yearning to belong compensated for the lack of lust. I wanted to be his. If I didn't fit in within the gay community, then sooner or later I would have to face the truth. I didn't belong in the straight world, or the gay world. I belonged in a different world altogether. But for tonight I would keep running. Keep dancing. Keep drinking.

I smiled at him and nodded. A new song started and I had moment of hesitation. Georgina came back in to dance and I grabbed her arm and pulled her into the hallway. Lee looked at me confused and I signalled for him to wait for a moment. He looked awkward, suddenly on his own, but nodded slowly.

Georgina was drunker than I was. I pulled her arm and we went upstairs to her bathroom. The tiles were a disgusting pink and there were actually rubber ducks on the bath. I sat frustrated on the toilet seat.

"Babe, what's wrong? You look proper down. Actually, you look a mess." She said bluntly.

"Georgina, something is wrong with me. I mean, like, really fucking wrong." My emotional barriers broke down to nothing.

"What do you mean?"

"Like my head. My head is messed up. Things aren't right. *I'm* not right." I put my head in my hands and then ran them through my short boyish hair. The mirror in front of me teased and tortured me, so I kept my eyes closed. "Sometimes I think I shouldn't have been born."

"What? No! Don't say that! What's brought this on? Is it Lee? Do you want me to ask him to leave you alone?"

"No, it's not that. Well, it's not just that. I think I should have been born a girl, Georgina." There, I said it. How will she react? Will she understand? Will she laugh?

"Right... I see. Well, I can see that within you, yeah." It was like she had sobered up in seconds.

"I'm sorry, this is all too much. I think I need some air." Her calmness freaked me out. It was like I had admitted defeat. Would I have to keep going down this road now? Had I finally admitted it to myself? I would be rejected from the straight community and lose my identity as a gay man too. I would be... nothing. I would cease to exist.

Her voice trailed off behind me as I escaped it all. I couldn't tell what she had said. I was running away. The music faded too. The smell of teenage sweat was replaced by fresh air. I went straight through the front door and out into the road. It was cool, dark and empty. Exactly what I needed.

The party continued, but I was finished. I looked at my watch. It was 3:17 a.m. – I was drunker than I thought. The world around me was spinning and my stomach churned. Georgina's friend's house was in the middle of nowhere. I decided to walk around to clear my head. It was all too much. I walked along the main road

163

until I came to a small alleyway. It led to a park not far from our school that I knew fairly well. It was probably dangerous to go down there alone on a Friday night, but alcohol and self-anguish clouded my better judgement.

Luckily it was empty. Even criminals weren't out at this time. Only me. I was alone here. All alone. Where should I go? Home? That would be the sensible option. It was only a few minutes from here. But no. That was no good, I just wanted to be out. But without a direction to walk in, what would I do? I would probably end up sitting somewhere and overthinking everything. So with panic still in my heart, I decided to walk towards Karl's house. Then, when this horrible feeling passed, I would head home. It would be hours before I was safe in my bed, but that didn't matter.

The walk was peaceful. I cleared my mind and only thought about which foot to put forward next. It was simple. Easy. Blissful even. Karl's house came into sight, although it was shrouded in darkness. I didn't think he would be in. He was probably out drinking. It didn't matter, I didn't want to talk to him. We would have our holiday to chat about stuff. Maybe I would tell him about tonight, or maybe I wouldn't.

As his house got smaller and smaller behind me, I headed towards my house. Probably only another two hours to go. Were my parents still up? Probably not. I could just sneak home as if this never happened. Georgina rang and I said I was fine. Everything was fine. The night was finished. This episode was over. Time to escape into my dreams. Escape from this confusion. Escape from everything.

* * *

Karl's car pulled up the drive. It was already getting dark. I quickly ran out and found a bush to pee in. My body stopped shaking as a wave of relief went over my body.

"Couldn't you have waited until we got inside Eric?" Karl called out as he grabbed our bags from the car boot.

"Sorry! It's been hours, I couldn't hold it any longer." I yelled from the bushes. Karl laughed to himself and walked up to the front door. His footsteps made a loud crunching sound on the gravel driveway. I wiped my hands on my jeans and met him by the door. "Is that all of it?" I asked.

"Yep. Can you lock the car?" Karl passed me the keys. The cottage was entirely covered in ivy and looked tiny. The driveway was so long that it disappeared from sight into the forest. There were birds that you don't hear in the suburbs of London. Insects that sounded like they came from another planet. We were cut off from city life and cocooned in Mother Nature's hands.

I walked through the door. Karl was in the bathroom. Our bags were on the sofa in the middle of the open-plan living room and kitchen. The cottage seemed much larger on the inside than it had from the outside. The two bedrooms were on the right, with the bathroom in the middle. Karl was peeing with the door wide open. The bathroom was small, but it did have a lovely bath. I couldn't wait to have a nice bubble bath, with a glass of wine and just relax in there. There was also a real fireplace in the middle of the main wall in the front room. It had a wooden shelf high above it. The wood was thick and polished. On it was a selection of blue pots and candlesticks.

On the counter in the kitchen, there was a bottle of red wine, a freshly made cake and an A4 booklet. I grabbed two glasses from the cupboards, poured the wine and began to read. It was mostly what we had seen online. No smoking, no pets, no children. None of those would bother me, but Karl would have to smoke in the garden. Oh, the garden! I hurried to the back door to the left of the cottage and peered through the window with my glass still in hand. It was dark now, so I could barely see anything, but it looked full of plants.

"Oh, nice." Karl walked over and grabbed his glass of wine. "Here's to getting no schoolwork done!" He clinked his glass against mine. I smiled and took a sip. I felt like an adult.

"It's lovely here! I can already feel myself unwinding." My eyes darted around the beautiful rustic decor. I walked over to the antique leather sofa.

"Same." Karl never usually spoke much and I could tell he was tired from the driving.

"How about I sort us out something to eat. You go and chill or something." I put my glass down and looked in our shopping bags.

"No, don't be silly. I'll help."

"Honestly, Karl, it's fine." I put the ingredients to make a chilli con carne to one side and put the rest of the shopping away. I couldn't wait to test out the large cottage kitchen.

"Eric, are you sure? I'm a bit shattered after driving all that way. I would love to just stick something on and relax." I could see the tension leave his shoulders.

"Go sit down. It won't take me long." I busied myself in the kitchen, which was pretty amazing. It had a large oven with six stoves. Ours at home only had four.

I diced, chopped, stirred and poured. Everything was simmering nicely. The heat from the garlic bread rose into the air as I pulled it out of the oven.

"Eric, that smells amazing." Karl called out without looking round. He was transfixed on an action film. I agreed to watch that as it would probably have some hunk that I could watch running about with guns while I ate my dinner. I brought the trays over and sat down on the other side of the large sofa. We didn't sit close to each other.

"Thank you. Thank you so much." He paused the film just to thank me. His eyes looked at mine. He smiled and clicked play. I grinned back and settled into the sofa. The smell of dinner rose from my lap and I started to eat. I should have added more herbs and left the rice to cook for a bit longer.

"Fuck me, this is awesome!" Karl shouted out.

"Glad you like it" I said proudly. Of course, I did love him. He was everything I wanted. When I was with him I felt normal. Myself, but somehow more than myself.

The next day we went for a walk to explore the forest that surrounded the cottage and then the local shops. We had both slept well in our separate bedrooms. Karl said it made a change from having his three dogs running in at 5 a.m. and climbing on his bed.

The local shops were quiet and empty. I only saw elderly women strolling through the streets. That made us, two teenage boys, stand out more. We talked about how everyone back home thought we were a gay couple. I said it must look like that now, but Karl disagreed. He said that old people didn't even think like that. He probably had a point.

We took shelter from the floods of old people in a small coffee shop at the very end of the main row of shops. It was empty. There wasn't even anyone behind the counter.

"Hello? Anyone in?" Karl called out, letting out a small laugh at the situation. I hid behind him. The decor was beyond anything I'd seen before. Dusty brass metal pots and pans hung from the walls. A thousand cat ornaments and yet no cats. What even was this place? There was a nice picture above the counter though. It was an oil painting of a curly haired woman dancing.

"Coming!" A voice called from up the stairs that until then neither of us had even noticed. They were hidden behind the shelf behind the counter.

Eventually a man in his forties came down and we ordered something to eat and drink. He brought it to us, only to climb back upstairs. We hadn't even paid yet.

"Wow, this is different to London, right?" I said to Karl.

"Totally. So random." He sipped his tea. For a moment we sat quietly. "Are you alright Eric? You seem a bit distant. You have this whole trip actually." That shocked me. I thought I was acting normal. I was always the one talking, yet somehow he could tell.

"Well, I guess I have some stuff on my mind. Just general stuff, but I'm ok."

"Come on, I know you want to talk. Just tell me."

"It's nothing new Karl. You know me better than anyone. We've been friends now for years."

"Oh, is it about us?" He looked down guiltily. "Eric, you know I'm straight. We're close friends and that's how I like it."

"No! God no, it's not that." I chuckled from shock. "You know me right?"

"How do you mean?"

"So like, at the party on Friday, I ended up leaving halfway through. I just went for a walk. I just had to get out. I walked for hours, all over the place. I just spent the whole time imagining stuff. I have this like, imaginary best friend. She's a strong woman and can do anything she wants. Sometimes, when I was younger I imagined her walking home with me. She has long hair and is just amazing." Karl nodded slowly. "I guess... I'm imagining a woman. I think... I just want to be one."

"That must be tough. Like, I can't imagine not wanting to be me. Sure, I wish I had a bigger dick I guess." He shrugged his shoulders and laughed at himself. I could tell he was trying hard to understand. Soon our teacups were empty. "A part of me does see you as a girl though. You know that. It's just hard, right? You're Eric. You're a boy." He paused. His tone changed. "You don't think you'll change one day, do you?"

"No, no way. It's just not that easy, is it? I couldn't do something that drastic. Think of how tall I would be. I'd be a fucking monster if I tried to turn into a woman." I laughed. Karl did too. It was a mix of awkward laughter and relief from the tension.

That was enough of that conversation. I started talking about what we would have for dinner and the rest of the day flowed normally. The greenery on the way back was beautiful. The forest seemed to go on forever once we were inside it. Broken twigs cracked under our feet. Animals could be heard but not seen. Our shoes got heavy and dirty. We found ourselves very hungry and ready for another night of chilling, watching films and listening to music together.

Winter had given way to soft breezes and light showers. In the afternoon it was even warm. Spring was here. Time was going by and with each day that passed, I was developing into the woman I wanted to be. I was happier and I was adjusting well to my new life.

Georgina and I had grown even closer. We didn't need to talk to communicate our thoughts and we lived completely in sync. Most of our Sundays were spent shopping together and in the evenings we tried on new outfits while eating ice cream. The arguments had stopped and there was no tension between us anymore.

My hair was getting long enough to hide my face when I put my head down. I often curled it, which made me look feminine and trendy. I noticed some guys were even starting to pay me attention. I could only assume that if that was the case, it meant that I was passing as a woman. It filled me with so much hope. I felt empowered. Like anything was possible.

It was Tuesday and the restaurant was quiet. I pulled a few pints, uncorked some bottles of wine and opened several cans of soft drinks. I let my mind wander, as I wiped down the bar. I always made sure to clean up the area I'd been working in. Regardless, there was always something to tidy. It probably had something to do with Paul hiring a bunch of messy teenagers. I wasn't much older, but I guess I was just about old enough to understand the importance of tidying up after yourself. The team was mostly made up of university students. Understandably, none of them treated this job as a career. I wouldn't have if I was them.

But for me it was different. I had really grown attached to this place. The owner, albeit slightly old-fashioned in his way of thinking, was a kind and sweet old man. Paul always looked after me. Alysha was a close friend. Ellie had come into herself and wasn't so clumsy anymore. The whole team had really bonded.

After the incident with Alex, I also got a lot more respect from the kitchen staff. Some regulars called me by my name and knew all about my situation. I could see myself settling down here and maybe even taking it over one day.

Paul had once told me that he had no intention of buying the business after the owner died. He told me how long he thought the old man had left. It was a slightly morbid conversation that only happened after a very long and busy shift and three or four whiskeys.

"I love this place, I do. But I never wanted to run a place like this. My passion isn't in serving food, it's cooking it."

"So why not look at becoming the chef one day?" I asked. Paul grabbed me a glass and I poured myself a small whiskey. I hated spirits, but he clearly wanted to talk and I liked being treated like an adult.

"It's not as simple as that B." Sometimes he used my old nickname instead of Fiona. I didn't mind. "We have a good head chef. There is no way I would fire him and take over. I also wouldn't be able to cook alongside him. He's great at what he does but hard work to get on with. Plus, I don't want to cook Italian food. I love French cuisine." He was a very gentle guy and I wondered if he had someone in his life. He never mentioned anyone.

"Oh I see. I thought you were content here. But even if it's not exactly what you want in the future, it's a great place to be for now, right?"

"That's true I guess. But actually, I have some money saved. Some inheritance money. I'm just biding my time here until the moment's right. One day I'll find a partner, settle down and start my own French restaurant. Probably not in Central London though. I'll find somewhere in the suburbs." He smiled as he pictured it in his head.

"Well, I hope that dream becomes reality. You'll make a great chef, I'm sure."

I started to wonder about the partner he mentioned. Paul never normally spoke about that kind of stuff. Alysha said he must be bisexual as she had seen him out on dates a few times with both men and women. A bisexual partner would make things so much easier for me. But as nice as he was, I could tell he wasn't my type. That thought alone made me realise something. I had grown up a lot as a person. Before, I would just have gone out with anyone who fancied me. I wanted to feel loved. I wanted to feel special. But now it was different. Even if Paul told me he loved me, I would say sorry, but no. He wasn't my type. Perhaps that was normal, but for me it was progress. Proof that I was settling into the real me.

The slow Tuesday night continued. My mind would have wandered further into the past had it not been for a sudden fairly large drink order. A party of four were clearly here to drink, rather than eat. They each ordered a different cocktail and a bottle of house red for the table.

As I cut the fresh lemon and shook the alcoholic mixes, Alysha came over to the bar area. She was in no rush.

"Hey girl, ya'll right?" She asked.

"I'm good babes, bit bored. Today is dragging."

"I know, right! Like, what the fuck? Did you get my drink order for table ten?"

"Yeah, I'm on it now. The cocktails are ready if you want to take them first? I'll follow behind with the wine in a second."

"Ok, thanks. No rush though, as two of them are out smoking anyways."

"Oh right, well, whenever you're ready." I said as she nodded.

"So B, how have you been, girl? You and that Karl guy doing ok?" She rested on the bar. I loved her as a friend, but it could be frustrating working with her since she was quite lazy. I didn't mind tonight because it was so dead.

"We're ok. He's so sweet."

"But…" She grinned and leaned in to get the gossip. I laughed and leaned in over the bar too.

"I don't know, something seems wrong. All too good to be true maybe?"

"How come? Did you tell him about those dreams you've been having?"

"No, I've not told him about those yet. Although they are still happening. Recently they have been building up. It feels like something big is coming. Really big. Like it's all coming to an end."

"Oh, so it's the trans thing. Do you guys even have sex?" She whispered to me.

"Alysha! I am far too sober for that conversation." I laughed.

"Girl, then hit us up with some work juice. I wanna know." She joked.

"Ok, well, I'll tell you." I gave in. "We barely kiss. It's been weeks of dating now. We snuggle, cuddle and all that stuff. But we never actually do more. I worry that he doesn't find me attractive in that way. Maybe he's scared?"

"Well that can't be it. Boys don't date girls they don't find attractive, what's the point?" She shrugged her shoulders.

"So then, what is it?"

"Maybe he's just trying to be a gentleman. Don't complain that your guy is being too nice, girl. Damn." We laughed together and she put her arm around me. "Now I better go and serve. You get to work on finding us something to drink, ok B?" She grabbed the tray. "This day is boring as fuck right now."

"You're terrible, Alysha!" I followed her with the wine and four glasses on. "I'll see what I can do."

* * *

173

Karl put his arms around me and I sank into them. We were sitting in a corner of a pub down the road from my flat. We were happy and things were going well, or at least that's what I let everyone believe, including Karl.

If I had known a couple of years ago that I would make it this far and one day be sitting in a pub, on a Wednesday night, with a gorgeous guy, living as a woman, I would have cried with happiness. He was confident, caring and charming. I felt safe and secure around him. Our first kiss was on our second date after eating together at my restaurant on my day off. Alysha brought us a surprise bottle of Prosecco and we both let the bubbles go to our heads. That night, after making sure I got home safely, we stood outside my flat and he asked me to be his girlfriend.

And yet, like I had told Alysha, I couldn't shake the feeling that it was too good to be true. He was a genuine and lovely guy. He had grown up a lot since secondary school. But a part of me didn't feel confident enough to be with him.

As I sat with Karl, I thought back to the other night when I had been on my own in the flat. I had been drinking too much wine and found myself thinking about our relationship long and hard. Whenever we were out together I could feel people staring. Their eyes followed me. Our every movement was being watched. In every restaurant, every cinema, every club. He didn't seem to notice, but I could tell. People stared at us constantly. I had finally become the woman I was destined to be, and yet this was a clear sign that I was yet to pass fully. The smirks, the sneers and the shouting. I was still a trans woman in everyone's eyes. And that undermined everything I had achieved so far. Just when I was feeling confident, just when I thought I was finally 'finished', some stupid idiot would heckle me in the street and bring my confidence crashing back down. There were only so many times that Karl could throw them against the wall in my defence without it getting serious.

That was why it was so horrible. I sipped the chilled Chardonnay slowly. I loved him. I had loved him since we first met in secondary school all those years ago. I was so happy that he was back in my life. But I felt so bad for him. If people were staring at me for being a 'tranny', then what on earth did they think of him? A pervert? A chaser? The thought of that filled me with guilt. I could feel it forming a barrier between us.

When he tried to kiss me in public, I would turn away shyly. My eyes were on the floor, so that my hair covered them and my hand hovered over my chin. What else could I do? I had to hide from the eyes that were on us. But I couldn't do that forever. Would I be fifty years old, and still nervous to be out in public? Would this ever change? It was this fear and this guilt that got between us. I tried my best to hide it, but I'm sure Karl could tell.

The pub we were in was dark and stuffy. We both liked it though. It was cosy and easy to relax in. I so wanted to let myself be happy. I wanted him to be happy. His hand caressed my arm gently and I closed my eyes for a small moment.

"Fancy another?" He asked me, slowly sitting up.

"Sure. You're ok for time?" I asked. He had a fairly long journey back.

"Yeah, I'm in no rush."

"Ok baby." I smiled, drank the rest of my wine and passed him the glass. He came back with more drinks, sat back in the same corner of the bench and I rested my head back on his shoulder. He squeezed me with his left arm and sipped his beer with his right.

"So, Fiona, I had something I wanted to ask you." He turned to me with a craned neck. My face was too close to his for him to look at me normally, so I sat up.

"Sure, what's up?"

"You remember my sister, right?"

"Julie, yeah sure. What about her?"

"So, she's getting married next week. Until now I figured I'd have no one to bring. But, I really like you and I was wondering if you wanted to come with me. Most of my family know you anyway. Well, kinda." He chuckled, and pinched my cheeks lightly.

"Karl, that's... that's really sweet, but are you sure?"

"I like you a lot. I've known you for years, so it doesn't feel like we've only been dating for a few weeks." His eyes locked on mine and I could feel him reading every movement I made. I sipped my wine to give me time to think. He drank his beer.

It was a big thing he was asking me. His sister's wedding? Everyone would be there. Hundreds of people. His mother. Oh no, his mother. What would she say? Do they know about me? I didn't know if the thought of him having told everyone was worse than not having told anyone yet. I felt a wave of anxiety rush over me so I closed my eyes.

"I want to, I do. I'm just a bit nervous. Everyone will be there. What will they say?"

"Fuck what they say. Fiona, you look beautiful. Who cares what people think? I've told you, it doesn't bother me, so it shouldn't bother you." He said honestly. But I couldn't believe him. How could I believe him? I was a monster. I started to freak out. I had to get out of the pub and be on my own. "Fiona, calm down. Look at me." I looked at him. "Everything is going to be ok." He grabbed my hands and held them close to his chest. Maybe I could trust him. Maybe people wouldn't notice.

"But what if people stare?"

"I've told you a million times. They aren't staring because they can tell you're trans. They're staring because you're a tall, beautiful and striking woman. I'm proud to have you by my side. Look, if you weren't passing as a woman, I wouldn't be with you, would I?"

176

In a moment of emotion he said it. There it was. It was such a backhanded compliment. I didn't want to let myself get upset, but I couldn't help it. So if people *could* tell I was transgender, he wouldn't want to be with me? But that was what I'd been telling myself all this time. It was understandable and yet so painful. It just hurt to hear him say it. I drank more. I wanted to go home and eat ice cream with Georgina. "Ok, I know that sounded horrible, but you know I mean it in a nice way. You don't have to worry baby, you look fine. Better than fine. You're gorgeous just the way you are." He was trying to soothe me, but his words were tainted. But how could I lose him? Again. After everything.

"Ok, I'll go. I'd love to go. I will literally need the entire morning to get ready though. I will need my nails done and hair curled. Everything." I planned it in my head as I spoke.

"Whatever you want Fiona. It's gonna be fun, I promise." He smiled and kissed my forehead.

* * *

On the day of the wedding I woke up at 5 a.m. to start getting ready. It was a Saturday, so I had to ask for the day off work. I checked the mirror for the seventh time that hour. My hair was short and curly. I had fake nails that matched my outfit. I wore a maxi dress, which covered me from top to bottom and a tight black cardigan on top. To be totally safe, I wore three pairs of tight knickers underneath it all.

"God your body is really starting to change, Fiona." Georgina called as she saw me through my open door. It was true. My hips were wider and my boobs were closer to a B cup now. Today I had a padded bra too though. I was so used to covering up in winter that I hadn't really noticed quite how much my body was changing. Finally it was spring and I could show off my new feminine curves.

"Thanks hun. I'm so nervous!" I called back. She was in the bathroom now, but could still hear me.

Karl would be outside in his car any minute. I was as ready as I would ever be. I practised my smile and it made my face look much more feminine. Also, if I raised my eyebrows it made the masculine protrusion that was my forehead look smaller. My nose was massive, but all I could do to change that was contour it with makeup. Karl made me promise that I would wear minimal makeup though, as he told me that I looked better that way.

I heard the car horn outside.

"I gotta go. See you tonight!" I shouted to her again.

"Wait! Let me see you properly!" She called out from the toilet. The door opened as she forced it with her toes, so she could see me.

"Georgina, you're disgusting." I said, as I saw her sitting there. "Do I look ok?"

"Fiona, fuck me, you look stunning. I wish I had your hips. And look at that booty – I'm so jealous!" I laughed and made my way downstairs.

When Karl saw me, his eyes widened and his mouth dropped. He got out of his car, even though it was a busy road with nowhere to park.

"Wow, Fiona, you look amazing. Your hair, your eyes. I..." He went to say something, but then stopped himself. I couldn't tell what it was. My heart was racing too much. I had never been out with so few layers on. I held a shawl, along with my handbag, over my right arm for the evening. Other than that, I was just wearing the dress and the cardigan. I was covered up and yet my shape was on show.

"Are you sure about this?" I gave him one last chance to back out.

"More sure than you could know. Fiona, I'm really glad you're back in my life. When we were young... I

know a lot happened. I know it was confusing. But...
I..."

"Come on, we should get going. We have to be there for 1 p.m., right? It's a long drive." I brought his focus back down to today.

"You're right. We only have three hours to get there." I walked round to the passenger's side and opened the door. I felt like a true Princess. I sat down in his car and took a breath. I glanced up at the flat to see Georgina staring down and waving energetically. I smiled back.

He looks hot in a suit. A message from Georgina flashed up on my phone. It was true. He looked more handsome than I had ever seen him. He still had a thick ear piercing in and his tattoo showed through his collar all the way up along his neck. But he was cleanly shaven and his hair was gelled neatly to one side. It felt like I was living the dream. It was everything I had ever wanted. I just hoped it wasn't all too good to be true. I prayed tonight didn't somehow end up in tears.

We talked and laughed for three hours. The busy city of London fell away and was replaced by churches, fields and forests. Elderly couples were walking their dogs on the muddy paths and cows chewed on grass in the distance. It felt like Devon again. That made me realise how so much had changed and yet nothing had changed at all. We were two different people, but at the core of it all, we connected. It was easy being around him. Simple. It felt right.

While Karl drove I had plenty of time to check my makeup in the car mirror. By the time we arrived we were slightly late and the ceremony was just about to start. There was only time for waves of hello and the odd kiss on the cheek from closer relatives. The groom was ready in the main hall and we were seated with Karl's family on the bride's side. Everyone was focused on her. She was tall and blonde. Her hair curled down around her, followed by a flowing white dress. She looked like a deity of love. Her smile lit up the room as she walked down the aisle.

"You alright?" Karl whispered into my ear as the hall fell silent.

"I actually am." I said and I kissed him on the cheek. He looked deep into my eyes and squeezed my hand. Everything felt magical. I felt like I could finally start trusting him and let myself be happy.

The day went on as most weddings did. The ceremony, the speeches, the music. Drunk uncles danced by the bar and young boys slid across the wooden hall on their knees. Karl and I kept away from the spotlight and watched the night unfold. Then the moment of truth came. Karl's mother had finally broken away from the bride and came to our table.

"My darlings, how are you?" She said. She placed her glass down on the table and sat next to me. Karl was on my other side.

"Hello mum, everything going smoothly?"

"Yes, it really is. Julie has never been so happy." She said. She was talking to me, not Karl.

"Julie looks absolutely stunning today." I said, as confidently as I could. My hands were shaking with nerves, but Karl was holding them comfortingly.

"She's not the only one." She said slyly. Then it came, the moment of truth. "Fiona, is it? You look beautiful." My heart was racing. Karl's was too. I could feel his pulse through our hands. "It suits you, ya know. A lot. I'm very happy for you."

That was it. It sounded genuine. She smiled, got up and walked over to the next table to talk to more distant relatives. Was that ok? Did it go ok? Karl exhaled heavily and took a sip of water.

"I think that went... well?" I said, unsure how Karl was feeling.

"It did! Thank god. I was petrified. My mum is known for saying whatever she wants." He said.

"So... she knows it's me, right?" I had to check.

"Yeah, she knows. I told her about you the moment I saw you at the restaurant. She wasn't shocked either. I don't think she thought we'd starting dating though." He laughed to himself.

"I don't think any of us did." I joked. He laughed again.

The hardest part was over. If Karl's mum was ok, no one would have the guts to go against her. I was accepted by her, and therefore by Karl's family. In a blaze of confident glory, I made my way to the toilets to freshen up.

I sat down in the cubicle as the toilet doors opened again and two giggling girls walked through it.

"And did you see Christina? Jesus, she's piled on the pounds!" They cackled amongst themselves.

"I know! She was hovering around the cake like a bee around honey."

My body froze. I couldn't leave the cubicle until they had gone. But at the same time, it would be weird if I sat here the whole time. Maybe I could check my makeup in here and then quickly rush to the sinks, splash my hands and get out before they properly noticed me.

"And Karl's girlfriend... Fuck me, she is massive."

"I know right! And she's dressed like a librarian. Have you heard the rumours?" They lowered their voices.

"Heard them? Who hasn't! Fucking sick if you ask me. Who knew Karl was some sort of pervert? I expected better of him. I saw him kiss it earlier and I was nearly sick at the table." They laughed even louder.

I had two options. Hide in here until they left, or walk out now and confront them. A part of me was ready for a fight. I was tipsy enough. They deserved it. Then I heard them each enter a cubicle. The path was clear. I could just get back to Karl and it would be over. Karl. Poor Karl. I felt the guilt rush over me. My poor, poor Karl.

181

I flushed the chain and walked quickly to the mirrors. What was even the point anymore? What did it matter about my makeup? I had to go. I had to get home. Karl would surely understand that I didn't want to be here anymore. But, I didn't want to tell him about any of this. Before I could get out of the toilets, another woman entered. She smiled at me and went straight into the cubicle. I ran out of the toilet.

Karl was still at the table, watching everyone enjoy themselves as the music continued. Old eighties classics.

"Everything ok baby? You were gone a while." He grabbed my hand again. "Fiona, have you been crying?"

"No, no. I'm fine. Getting kind of tired though, do you think we could make our way home soon?" I tried to steady my voice. More tears were a moment away, I could feel it. My stomach was cramping with nerves and my body felt hot and stiff. My heart was broken. I knew what I had to do.

"What? It's not even 8 p.m. yet." He looked confused, but he could tell something was up. "But if you want to go, we can go. Let me just make the rounds and say goodbye to everyone, ok? Julie and Evan will probably be on their way to their honeymoon soon anyway." He tightened his tie and checked his hair in the mirror on the wall behind us. He really was very handsome. I loved him, but I couldn't carry on knowing what people thought of us. I wasn't ready. It was all too good to be true. I had known it all along.

As Karl made his way around the room, the two bitches from before came out from the toilet. They looked over to me sitting there on my own and laughed to each other. It wasn't their fault. They were young teenage girls. They would have made fun of anyone. I picked up the favour that was gifted to me. It was a small pink candle with a ribbon around it. Karl had personalised cufflinks. The candle smelled of roses. I tried my best to keep calm and smile.

"Come on then, let's head back." Karl said from behind me. He grabbed his jacket. I grabbed my bag. My movements were slow and cautious. It was dark outside. As I was aware of what I was about to do, I held tightly on to Karl's arm for what would be the last time. I should have known that this wouldn't work. I should have gone with my gut instinct.

We sat in the car, but Karl didn't start the engine. He just sat and stared at me.

"Are you ok? What happened?" His face was full of concern.

"I can't talk about it yet. We have a long drive ahead of us. I don't want to cry all the way home."

"Cry? Why? What happened? I thought it went well." He sounded confused.

"Please, Karl. Let's just get home. I don't want to talk about it now." I found myself shouting. I was angry, yes. But not at him. I felt even more guilt, but it was too late. He angrily reversed out of the parking space and drove off hastily into the country lanes. The journey seemed to last forever. We drove in silence. I looked out of the window, so that he couldn't catch my eye.

"So come on, what's wrong? I thought my mum was fine. I thought everything was fine." Karl finally pushed me enough to speak. I told him about the girls in the toilets. I told him what they said and how disgustingly horrible it made me feel. He was shocked, I could tell. His eyes were fixed on the road and his hands were tight around the steering wheel.

"That's why... Karl... I think we should stop seeing each other." I had finally said it. He froze. I looked away from him and back out at the passing buildings. Tall skyscrapers stood in the distance mocking me. I was on the verge of tears.

"I don't want to stop this. Fiona, I really like you. A part of me always has."

"But don't you care what people are saying about us? They're literally laughing at us, Karl. At you." I felt anger erupt inside me. I couldn't deal with the guilt on top of my own insecurities.

"Fuck them, I don't care. Well, I mean, I do care. But... I don't know. It's complicated." He shook his head and I could see tears filling his eyes. He choked them back better than I ever could. Buildings blurred past us as the car reached a dangerous speed.

"Karl, I love you. You probably know that already. I've loved you since we were in year 8. I love you enough to not want to see the people around you laughing at you behind your back. Will it always be like this? In ten years, are we going to be celebrating our wedding? What will people say then? I can't give you children. I won't have my surgery for years still. I can't be the woman you deserve. I love you enough to want you to be happy." He broke down in tears. It was rare for him to cry so openly. Somehow, as sad as I was, I couldn't cry anymore. I had turned cold and angry at having to do this. It wasn't fair. It was like there were no tears left.

"Fiona, don't do this. I..." He looked at me quickly. He was still driving, so he couldn't stare into my eyes, like I could tell he wanted to. "Fiona, I care about you so much. When we were younger I guess I somehow liked the girl inside you. I didn't know it then, not properly. But I know it now. You're back in my life now as the girl you should have always been. Surely that means we should be together." Tears fell down his face as he realised that I had made up my mind.

"I love you Karl, I'm sorry. Maybe it will happen for us one day. When I've had my main surgery, and maybe even facial surgery. But not now. Not yet." I looked down at my lap, but I could still feel his eyes burning into me. The rest of the journey went by in silence. Neither of us spoke. Neither of us could.

"How about this one?" Georgina suggested. "It's long and black, I think it'll suit you."

"I don't know, it looks pretty heavy. I think it should have a fringe too." I replied.

"Ok, how about this one? It's the same wig, but with a full fringe. That will make your face look smaller." She held it out. My hand reached out and touched it. It felt soft and delicate. I had always dreamed of having long hair. Mine would take years before it grew to this length. Wearing a wig would be horrible and uncomfortable, but it meant I would look like a woman so I had to do it.

"Wait here, I'll go and try it on." I walked into the booth. The shop assistant stood behind the desk smiling at me and Georgina.

"Are you her girlfriend?" She asked Georgina. I in no way looked like a woman, but the assistant was used to transgender people coming in here. She knew how to address me.

"Oh, no, no! Just his best friend. Her! Sorry, *her* best friend." Georgina blushed. It had only been a week or so since I had told her it was official. She took it amazingly and hugged me right on the spot. I was blessed to have a best friend like her. She told me that we would go shopping over the weekend to buy everything we needed. Wigs, makeup, clothes. Then that night we would have a full on fashion show. I was so excited. It was like a dream come true. I had been hiding it for far too long.

"Georgina! How does this look?" I shouted out from inside the booth. She came around the corner and I stepped out. I still had stubble on my face and was wearing jeans and a hoody, but I had placed the wig on my head and adjusted it as best I could.

"Ok, yes. It looks... like you have long, black hair." She was honest. I looked like a boy in a wig. It would be a long time before I passed as a woman. It would be years before I had my own boobs and a body shaped like a girl's.

"Well, let's get this one and work on it tonight. I'm already getting hot underneath it." I took it off and sorted myself out. We paid for it and moved to the next shop. The assistant smiled with delight. It was kind of creepy.

"So Eric, what are you going to tell your family? Are you gonna pick a new name?" Georgina asked quietly as we walked along the main road with shops either side.

"I'm not sure about a name. That's so official. But I will tell my family soon. They deserve to know. I guess I'll need to go home."

"And work? What will your work say? You've only been there two weeks, right?"

"Yeah, but I don't think legally they can say anything, right? And it's not like I'm just going to suddenly turn up for work in stilettos with bright pink blusher on my face. I want to transition naturally. Take my time and do it right. I don't want to be a freak, Georgina. I can't take that." I thought about it as I spoke to her. It's true, work might be harder to tell than my family. But it had to happen. I had made my mind up. I couldn't keep running from the truth.

Next we bought makeup and clothes. I chose simple yet feminine stuff. Long pink t-shirts that went down to my thighs. Baggy cardigans that had long sleeves so I could pull them over my large hands. Scarfs that I could hide in when it was colder outside. I wasn't ready to buy long dresses or tights yet. Soon, but not yet.

We found a small place to have a bite to eat and then made our way home. It had been such a fun day out shopping with Georgina. Although the real fun began after that. We made it back to the flat, wiggled between unpacked cardboard boxes and headed straight for the bathroom. It was cramped in there with the two of us and all our shopping, but we made it work.

Georgina brought out some ice cream and two Mojitos. She said it was a celebration of rebirth, so there had to be cocktails. I took one sip and nearly gagged from the amount of alcohol in it. Georgina had never been any good at mixing cocktails, however much she tried.

First I shaved. It wasn't like an everyday shave. I shaved downwards, towards my neck, then upwards towards my ears. I shaved across and diagonally. My fingers slid across the smooth skin to feel for any leftover bumps. When I reached some I would shave over that bit again. Again and again, I sliced away the illness that grew on my face every day. I hated shaving. I hated the act of it. It was so masculine. I hated the hairs themselves. The colour, the texture, the itching. It dawned on me that the process to get rid of hairs via electrolysis was both expensive and long. Three years down the line, I would probably still need to shave at least every other day.

Then I moisturised. My skin was bleeding and raw from shaving so close, so I used the strongest moisturiser I could find. It stung so bad I screamed out in pain and Georgina – feeling helpless – handed me the Mojito. I drank and grimaced until the pain wore off.

"That looks painful, are you alright? Should we wait before putting makeup on it?"

"No, it's fine. It's ok now. Just a bit red." Red bubbles started to appear on my neck. The hairs grew at such an awkward angle that cutting would surely cause a rash. I would need lots of foundation to cover it.

"Ok, then let's do this." Georgina grabbed the shopping bag full of makeup. At that point I barely knew what any of it was. She applied darker makeup to what felt like the outer areas of my face and lighter makeup in the centre. She drew thin lines along my nose. Then she seemed to be blending everything in, concentrating on my upper cheeks. I watched her in the mirror. I watched my own face slowly melt away under layers of oils and colour. Would this work? Would I look like a woman now? Doubtful.

"Next step – you do your eyes. This is mascara."

"Georgina, I know what mascara is."

"Oh right, of course you do. Ok, so apply this while I find you the right eyeliner colour." She went back into the bag after sipping the dregs of her drink. "Wow, Eric, your eyes are actually really beautiful. Do you pluck your own eyebrows?"

"Yeah, I've been doing them for a while now. They get so bushy otherwise." I explained.

"That's good. That makes my job easier then." We giggled together.

"Georgina... Thank you for this. I can't explain it, but I feel... I feel wonderful. I feel alive for the first time in my life." I suddenly felt the Mojitos taking hold of my emotions.

"Stop tearing up hun, I won't be able to do your eyes if you're crying." She welled up too, but tried to keep it together. We looked at each other and just smiled. This had been a long time coming.

Nearly an hour later and we were finishing off the finer touches. I went with lip-gloss instead of lipstick so as to not look too much like a drag queen. My eyes looked amazing, thanks to Georgina. I tried to do my own wings, but failed so badly she had to start from scratch. I had blusher on, but not too much. Georgina explained that it was more about having highlighter in that area these days. My eyebrows were thick, but sleek and feminine.

The final touch was getting changed and putting my wig on. I slid into my long pink top and kept my jeans on underneath. Girls wore jeans too. Then I put the wig on. It was heavy and black. My natural hair colour was nowhere near black, so I felt different already. I leaned forward and forced my head inside. I flipped back and the hair fell dramatically behind me into place. It hit my back and my shoulders. I had never experienced that before. It felt right.

Georgina stared at me. I stared at the mirror. My face naturally formed a pout. Turning my head from side to side, I analysed myself in great detail. I looked like Eric. Eric in makeup and a wig. It looked grotesque and wrong.

"Georgina, what do you think?" I said solemnly.

"Can I be honest?" I was ready.

"Of course." I replied.

"You actually look better than I thought you would." I looked at her surprised.

"What do you mean? Are you saying you think I look ok?"

"Well, I mean, you can tell. But you do look feminine. You already had a feminine face. Your lips are the perfect shape and your eyes really stand out. Sure, you have a big jaw, but the wig covers that. And your nose looks smaller, thanks to my amazing makeup skills!" She made an exaggerated vogue pose and laughed. "But just generally, you actually look ok." She sounded genuine. Could I trust her?

"Seriously? Do you think I can do this? Do you think this is the right choice?"

"Do I think you can do this? Yes, I do. Do I think it is the right choice? That, my darling, is entirely your decision. Judging by tonight, I imagine it's not going to be easy. But if it's what you want, I will support you. Every step of the way. Ok?" She grabbed my hands and held them tightly. Her eyes locked on mine and I felt myself overflow with love again.

"It's not what I want to do, it's what I need to do." I stood up and pouted again. With my hands on my waist, I looked at myself in the mirror one more time. My hair fell around me like a protective shield. I certainly was... striking.

A few weeks later I found myself in a pile of papers, books and clothes. The radio played loudly in my room. Strong and empowering female pop singers sang to me as I rifled through everything I owned. It was a Sunday, so I decided I would take the entire day to sort my life out. I made lists of lists and planned the next five years. I would be a successful, hardworking woman in a relationship by the time I was 25. Simple.

Georgina was in her room too, doing the same. Our doors were both wide open. The music reached every corner of the flat. The piles of stuff leaked out into the hallway between our rooms. We had read the book on how to "tidy your life back into shape", written by a Japanese lady. It really was life changing. I had more of a reason to do it though, as I was clearing out all of my old stuff.

My parents said I could keep whatever stuff I wanted back home. They were still adjusting to my life-changing decision, so they didn't mind getting to keep some of my old stuff at theirs. I was sitting in amongst all my old diaries and deciding what to do with them.

"Did you ever write a diary, Georgina?" I called out over the music.

"No! Not really." She called back.

My eyes didn't look away from the scribbles on the pages before me. A part of me would feel strange throwing them away and yet they were the 'old me', not the 'new me'. That was the kind of thing, I decided, that should stay with my parents. I wasn't ready to throw them out, but I didn't want to keep them. It was the same with school photos, certificates and all my old secondary school stuff. My eyes caught a glimpse of Karl's name as I went to put the diary down. It was the day we first met. I got my first level 5 detention. As much as I hated getting it, it meant I met Karl. I

wondered what he was doing. He probably ended up in jail or something. I had such a crush on him once.

"Ok, what's next?" I said to myself.

"What?" Georgina called back to me.

"Never mind." I went over to the piles of books and old drawings. I had hundreds of images of her. The character that I had long dreamt of. She was a powerful witch who could turn into a flaming phoenix. She wore chopsticks in her hair and only dressed in the finest gowns. Seeing this old artwork made me want to draw again. It all went into the 'keep' pile and so did my small box of colouring pencils.

"Hun, I don't know about you, but I'm getting hungry. Shall we order a pizza?" Georgina suggested. My eyes lit up, negating any need for a reply. She went on to order our usual. I stood up. I still had a lot to get through, but I was making progress. Between the two of us, we had filled seven black bin bags. It felt like a detox of my life. All my old stuff, junk and useless items would be gone, leaving only the things that made me happy. Anything boyish went straight into the 'discard' pile. I found that I didn't really own much stuff like that anyway. It's not like I had ever been a masculine boy. My main chest of drawers was decorated with candles, crystals and flowers.

Before I knew it, the pizza had arrived and we were sitting in our kitchen eating it. Georgina poured us a glass of orange juice each and I sorted out the plates. We both looked at the piles of rubbish to be thrown out.

"This is the only detox I know of where you can eat pizza!" Georgina joked as she took her first bite.

"I know right, it's brilliant!" I started eating too. My mind was full of thoughts about my life and what was next on my list of things to do. Choosing my name, starting on female hormone replacement therapy, getting electrolysis on my face. The list went on. It was extremely daunting. I was glad to have Georgina there with me every step of the way. She was like my guardian angel. Even when she didn't know it, she was saving me. She was looking after me. My heart was heavy with thoughts of doubt and fear of the unknown. She was my rock when I needed grounding. She was my role model. She was even a shoulder to cry on.

The next few days would be spent trying to implement the changes in my new life. I cried a lot when the fear got the better of me. I realised how unhappy I had actually been all these years. Maybe that was part of the detox. Maybe that was normal. For now all I could do was try my hardest. There was no manual for becoming a woman. No instructions. Even talking to other transgender people only made me realise how long the process would be and it freaked me out more. I had to travel down this road alone. It would be a battle against the rest of the world. And with big battles come big commitments and big decisions.

Prince Hikaru rode Kaze deeper into the Southern Desert. The sand was warm against his hooves. The sun was shining down like a beacon of hope in the sky. Autumn was here and with it the smell of rotting leaves. Behind Kaze was an army larger than Macha Land had ever known. Every clan from every species sent their willing to march together in the name of their Queen. Queen Fubuki. Kaze's proud owner.

The Four Guardians were the first to see the oncoming enemy. Agility sprinted ahead to scout the vicinity. Defence stepped back to guard his Prince. The battle was upon them. The air was thick with tension. The silence was profound. Prince Hikaru wanted to shout back to his troops and bid them prepare themselves, but he dared not raise his voice.

To the West roared the Windy Planes and to the East there was nothing but cliffs and sea. They had travelled all the way from the Northern regions where the Main Stage and the Lake glistened in the sunlight. All that was before them was the Southern Desert. This great land was to be their battlefield.

The winds picked up and the sands moved with it. Prince Hikaru climbed down from Kaze's saddle and gently pulled him forwards by his reins. Kaze moved slowly in fear. Hikaru would have done the same were an entire nation not watching him. The battle was imminent. Suddenly, after a single footstep, he felt the ground move beneath him. Hikaru looked down in fear and felt his stomach churn.

Hundreds of small creatures ran over the sandy hills before them. They seemed to spread as far East, as far West and as far South as the Southern Desert itself. There were too many for Hikaru to even see. He could never have imagined an army of this scale. Gnarly sand monsters swarmed the ground. The King of Truth's army was here and charging towards them. Prince

Hikaru grabbed onto Kaze's reins and leapt back onto the mount.

"Charge!" He shouted as he unsheathed his bastard sword high into the sky. Without a moment's hesitation, the ten thousand souls fighting for their Queen lunged forwards. The dark herd of moving leather and armour followed Prince Hikaru into battle.

The sand creatures were armed with sharp rocks and stones. Although their weapons were primitive compared to the advanced elven craftsmanship of Fubuki's army, they were being wielded by bloodthirsty beasts. Centaurs charged forward, cutting down streams of them, while the elven clans knelt down to cast their arrows across the sky. Faeries attempted to heal those on the front line that were already falling victim to attacks. They flew around them in circles emitting healing blue lights, but they too were succumbing to the horrors of war.

Kaze led the centaurs and penetrated into the heart of the battle. Hikaru slashed at the enemy, one by one as he rode over them. The stench of death and burning flesh was inescapable. They were now beyond the front line of the army of monsters. There were thousands and thousands of these creatures. Far more than anyone had expected. Kaze felt the slice of a rock against his back legs and produced a harrowing noise. His back legs weakened. He fell to the floor. Prince Hikaru was thrown into the warm dirt.

"Retreat! Retreat now!" Prince Hikaru yelled in panic. Retreating had been part of their battle plan as commanded by the Queen, but not this soon. Regardless, that was before anyone had a notion of how many they were facing. He knew it was too early, but Hikaru wanted to save as many of the innocent lives that were at stake as he could. There was no hope of winning this battle on the ground. They were outnumbered. Perhaps there was a way from the air, but he could not tell. He looked around helplessly as no one took heed of his orders. His words fell on deaf ears in the chaos as no one had expected orders of retreat yet.

Young dragonets flew above them, followed by scores of arrows sent by the elves. A small brown faery witnessed her Prince's turmoil and quickly flew to him. She dodged brutish punches and arrows as she did.

"By the powers of the Goddess, give his voice strength!" She spoke in a high-pitched, but compelling tone. With a splash of colourful energy, his throat suddenly felt bold and powerful.

"I said retreat! Now!" His voice boomed across the skies. Dragons and griffins stopped mid-flight and troops around him grimaced at the deafening sound. Those that could still retreat followed his orders and withdrew back the way they came. Their orders were to return back through the central pass between the Windy Planes and the edge of Macha Land on the East. This would draw the enemy into the thin passage and give them the means to chip away at the mass of enemies.

Kaze and Prince Hikaru were too deep within the enemy's forces to hope to escape. The faery who spelled her Prince's voice healed Kaze. Together they could only hope to fight their way to survival. He sat firmly on the horse's back, fighting off monsters as they struggled to ride away. The long katana glistened in the ever-burning sun and drew the attention of the enemies around him. Yet suddenly they stopped. The enemy was frozen still. Why? What was this trickery? He looked behind him and watched as Queen Fubuki's army retreated to the entrance of the passage. And yet the enemy did not follow. What were they doing?

In complete unison, every single one of the dusty beasts had stopped moving. Their small hunched bodies wrinkled up into balls. With weapons still in hand, they then pushed their bodies to the floor. Quickly, they began to bury themselves deep into the sands of the

Southern Desert. Within seconds they were underground. The desert seemed to swallow them whole. Those who were still on the battlefield tried to attack, but they were too slow. Sandy winds blew gently across the wasteland. Kaze edged backwards apprehensively.

Hikaru's heart pounded. Fear swept over him. He had his battle plans, but naturally so did the enemy. They had clearly only planned to get this far into the main island. After that it was a matter of time before they penetrated beneath the soft sandy floors. Now they had infested Queen Fubuki's precious island. They could be anywhere. And yet what worried Prince Hikaru most, was that he had seen neither his Queen, nor the King of Truth. They could be leagues away, fighting to the death.

Prince Hikaru dismounted once again to scan the area. A foul wind blew past him and he turned around. A man stood before him, roughly the same height. It was not the King of Truth, but someone else. A cloak of grey wool covered him entirely except for a lock of black hair identical to Hikaru's and a long curved blade. Slowly the stranger unsheathed his sword. Hikaru mirrored him.

They began to run at each other. Prince Hikaru dodged a horizontal strike by diving into a forward roll. The hood of his enemy fell from his head. Finding his feet, Hikaru's sword scraped against the stranger's, as he defended another attack. Were his eyes deceiving him? Was the heat getting to him? The strange man he was desperately fighting against with clash after clash of swords looked exactly like him. He was a darker, colder version of Hikaru. Each blow and kick that Hikaru dealt was met with equal strength. He was the perfect match.

The doppelganger's cloak fell clean off as Hikaru's sword sliced through his enemy's flesh. Blood trickled from his shoulder and down his chest. Angered, the enemy leapt out into a frenzy of furious blows against Hikaru. It pummelled him into the ground. His knees hit the burning sand. With all the strength Hikaru could gather, he fought the evil version of himself off with defensive strikes of his katana and kicked him away.

"Kaze, away! Find your Queen!" He ordered the mount to leave as he continued to deflect his ghastly foe. Silver metals hacked violently against each other, with no hope of an end. This man was surely the King of Truth's second in command. His most trusted ally. Only someone fighting for love would have this much strength. His passion seemed as strong as Prince Hikaru's for Queen Fubuki. Hikaru stepped back and focused his strength. He had been through worse than this. The deep depths of the ocean. The lost path in those everlasting woods. The forceful gusts of the Windy Planes. He was stronger after those trials. He was a better version of himself. He could defeat this doppelganger and get back to his Queen. He had to. It was his duty. A terrific strike of a sword fell down as Kaze galloped into the distance.

The main battle was far from over. It was not long since Kaze had last taken this same path from the Southern Desert to the capital. He would soon pass the Windy Planes and see the Main Stage and the Lake in the North.

As he galloped, he beheld the slaughter that had taken place. From the edge of the desert, all the way to the bottleneck of the passage he could see nothing but corpses. The smell was sickening. The land was bathed in red. Small muddy piles filled the paths and roads where the creatures had surfaced. Trees were on their sides. Faeries without their usual sparkle lay motionless on the floor. Elves were face down in the mud.

All the mount could do was look for his Queen. He lifted his heavy mane and looked ahead. He saw a peculiar red ball in what should have been a clear blue sky. It hurtled towards Macha Land leaving a trail of smoke and ash in its path. Kaze broke into a gallop as the ball of fire headed towards the Lake.

* * *

Queen Fubuki flew through the clouds, watching her army below her. Hundreds of her citizens had chosen to fight against this evil that threatened to take over the island. She had to protect them in return, as best she could. The King of Truth wanted to take her place. A King instead of a Queen. That couldn't happen. She was happy in her world. She was at peace. There had been peace here for all, before he came.

Hikaru's deep and bold voice echoed through the clouds around her. He had issued the order. She waited in the sky, slowly flapping her wings. She was the Phoenix now, ready to attack when the time was right. She was a ball of fire ready to explode.

She was watching, but nothing happened. The enemy didn't follow her army. Fubuki felt a wave of confusion. Fear gripped her heart. He knew. He knew everything. He knew her. Were they connected? She could sense somehow that they were.

Before Queen Fubuki had time to fly down and protect her people, a flock of blue ice birds came for her. Their feathers were as sharp as blades. Their beaks sharper still. They flashed in the sun as they flew in to attack the Queen. Blue met red in a whirlpool of agony. Fubuki felt freezing droplets searing her wings as she tried to fight them. It was no use. The pain was like nothing she had ever felt. It left her helpless to defend herself.

"Quaaa!" She screamed. With whatever power she could muster amidst the pain, she slapped the ice birds away with her wings. Steam engulfed her. Making use of this small moment of freedom, Queen Fubuki turned and made her way towards the Main Stage.

Hikaru...

With her thoughts on her beloved, she felt a frozen beak penetrate her fiery heart. The birds pecked at her burning wings and turned her magickal feathers to smoky ash, upon which, the Phoenix fell from the sky. She had to escape. She had to get away from these terrible creatures.

Her eyes were closed. Her power was being extinguished. The large ball of molten flesh crashed down towards the Lake.

* * *

"Your Queen is dead." The King of Truth announced to those remaining in Macha Land. They were forced out from their homes. Tied and bound. He stood in the centre of the Main Stage to address them. His voice was bold and proud. "She was no match at all." Held in the grasp of the ravenous sand creatures, the citizens of Macha Land had no choice but to listen to him.

"My people, my dear people. You have had an imposter on the throne for too long. I am your true King. I am the rightful leader of Macha Land. I am here to guide you into the new world. Where there is no freedom. No Justice. Only truth. While I rule, you will know not of love, or hate or pain. There is no need for it. Lovers, haters, fighters... You are all weak! Instead, I will give you real peace. A peace that can only be achieved with eternal slumber. Only death can bring an end to your pain. Follow me. I will lead you. Together, we will bring an end to your pain and suffering. As your new ruler, I command it. Follow me. Each and every one of you. Follow me!"

His words cut like knives into the hearts of the people of Macha Land. Their Queen was lost and their army slaughtered like cattle. He would turn her utopia into the underworld. There was nothing to fight for. There was no hope. Everything was lost.

A young girl dressed in simple linen, small enough to break away from the grasp of one of the beasts, ran towards the Main Stage. The crystal pillars of the stage stood tall before her. The sunbeams shone brightly through them.

"We won't do it! We don't want you. Go aw..." Suddenly, her voice was silenced. Her soul was set free from her tiny body, as a villainous creature cut her open. Those close to her gasped as she dropped silently to the floor. An innocent girl. One more soul lost in the battle that day.

The King of Truth was about to resume his speech when he was distracted by a bright light in the distance. The land fell silent as he strained to see what was blinding him. Then he caught a glimpse of red coming from below the Main Stage.

Kaze had reached her just in time. She was falling towards the Lake. In a splash of smoke and water, she hit the surface. But the Lake itself seemed to almost reject her. It was as if it was fighting for her to stay alive. Steam and smoke swirled around her, but she did not sink down. Instead, the surface of the Lake kept her afloat, and in doing so, stopped her eternal fire from being extinguished. Macha Land was with her. Kaze swam to her and pushed her to land. Still weak, she coughed and spluttered her way onto Kaze's saddle. Seeing the King of Truth on the Main Stage in the distance, she quickly rode Kaze to liberate her people.

Queen Fubuki, atop her noble mount Kaze, crashed down into him in a magnificent red whirl of fire. Kaze's hooves rammed into the King of Truth as Fubuki fell to the crystal floor. Shards scattered around the stage.

"No! Be gone!" He called out. His voice was powerful and garish. With it, Kaze disappeared into a cloud of black lightning. Queen Fubuki's hands reached out to him but it was no good.

"Kaze!" She cried. It was too late. The mount was gone. "Kono akuma wo toubatsu suru chikara wo kudasai!" Fubuki's ancient words filled the air. Pink smoke wrote the ancient alphabet in the air around her. She had been thrown from Kaze with great force, but she was ready. She had had enough.

The King of Truth faced her head on. He had no weapon. His hands were outstretched and ready to cast. He wore a black cloak and a frozen mercury crown. He looked upon her fiercely.

"Ready yourself, witch." He spat at her. She got to her feet and summoned her staff. She tried to summon Hikaru and her Four Guardians, but it was no use. Their location was blocked by a dark and bitter magick.

"You will never be King. I am the Queen! I am the ruler here! You will not take my kingdom. I will not allow it!" Her words were hoarse and tired. Emotion flowed through her body and she felt the magick within her work by itself.

A black bolt of lightning came flying her way, but she narrowly avoided it. She leant her head forward and squinted her eyes. With her hands in front of her, she conjured a ball of pure blue fire.

"Megami no chikari yo!" She shrieked. The burning blue flames soared towards the self-proclaimed King. He was summoning a bolt of his own, but still managed to dodge her flame. Fire met lightning as they circled each other atop the Main Stage. Light was flashing down upon the many citizens that were still being held hostage by the grotesque creatures of the wasteland.

Fubuki went to swirl her staff at the King of Truth, when he held his hands in front of him. He froze the air around him and the staff stopped mid-air. Without a moment's hesitation, Fubuki abandoned her staff and leapt towards him, conjuring her swords. White light grew from her hands and turned to metal.

"You will not kill me with metal, you stupid woman." He said to her as she hurtled towards him. "Metal turn to dust. Dust to ice." He said in a calm and steady tone. His hands seemed to grip around the swords that were thrust towards him. The blades shattered into a thousand pieces and fell to the floor.

Avoiding the shards on the floor, Queen Fubuki soared towards him again – her left knee bent against her chest and her right leg outstretched behind her. She reached out towards him and grabbed onto his black cloak. This time she was able to force him to the floor.

"Quaaaaaa!" She screamed violently in his face. Her voice was piercing. The King grimaced and covered his ears in pain. Now was her chance. Fubuki reached for her hip. With a final swipe, she plunged her small, red dagger deep into the King of Truth's chest. He drew a long and difficult breath. The King's hands wrapped around hers and his eyes widened with disbelief.

"No..." He choked. She just stared him in the eyes.

"Kill this evil and let it be known,
None will ever take my throne.
The magick of Macha, the face of war,
I bid this evil be no more!"

With her words, a wondrous light started to shine from the wound in his heart. It burst out with great power and spread across the stage. Dusty beasts with sharp weapons soon turned to piles of lifeless sand and the skies in the distance went from purple to the familiar blue. A wave of power and energy swept through the entire island. Citizens broke free and ran towards their loved ones.

Queen Fubuki knew deep down nothing would be the same. Yes, she had killed him. The King of Truth was no more. But her people had still been slaughtered by the thousands and her beloved mount was gone forever. Hikaru was surely dead as well. All she could do was hope. She had to be strong. She was still the ruler. She would do whatever it took to get the realm back to normal. She was still the Queen.

I finished late from work the night before, so I spent the morning sitting in bed. Usually I would have my butterfly pyjamas on, but it was too warm for that. I sat there in just my knickers and a bra top. My room seemed so much bigger since cleaning it out a few weeks before. I even managed to make space for a fan, which was whirling in the background.

Even though it was early summer, I still had a cup of tea and biscuits. I snuggled into my cushions, and watched my favourite programme. Romantic lovers flirted with each other on screen and made me drift off into a lonely daydream. I wanted that. I wanted a family of my own. It would be hard for me to get what I wanted, but I had to try. The world is full of all kinds of people – who's to say what's impossible.

Naturally I thought about Karl. I missed him so much. I had cried over breaking up with him for a long time after his sister's wedding. It hurt more that I hadn't spoken to him since. I had blocked his number, but still knew it off by heart. In moments of weakness – and drunkenness – I sometimes played with the idea of calling him. But what would it achieve? We were never going to work out. He deserved someone better than me. I deserved someone who understood me. Someone else trans maybe? A trans male would be someone I could be completely myself with. Not Karl.

Outside, I heard Georgina fumbling about. She was creeping outside my half opened door. She had been off sick on Friday because of a hangover. I wasn't sure, but I didn't think she had fully recovered yet.

"You ok, Georgina? What are you up to out there?" I asked.

"Nothing!" She called back. Her voice was still fragile.

Eventually she came into my bedroom with a tray in her hands. On the tray was a bacon sandwich and a bottle of ketchup. She stood in the doorway grinning.

"Is that for me?" I asked with glee.

"Yep!" She sat down at the end of my bed and placed it in front of me. I leant up and gave her a hug carefully over the tray. Gulping down my tea from before, I made a deliberate 'mmm' sound. Georgina laughed.

"Ok, so what did I do to deserve this then?" I picked up the sandwich and jokingly examined it.

"Well, I wanted to ask you a small favour." She suddenly seemed serious and looked me straight in the eyes.

"Anything. What's up? Are you ok?"

"I was wondering if you could tide me over until I get paid next week. I have had loads of birthdays to sort out recently and kind of lost track of my finances. It's just until I get paid, and then I can give it straight back." She buried her face in her hands. She was so sweet.

"Georgina, look at me." I grabbed her hand and forced her to look at me. "You are my best friend, and I love you. If it wasn't for you, I probably wouldn't be here. Of course I can help. Don't be silly. How much do you need? Whatever it is, just tell me and it's done." I picked up my smartphone so I could transfer the money into her bank straight away. I honestly didn't mind at all. The way she was acting had made me think she was going to ask something a lot more difficult. I had been working as a part of the management team at the restaurant for a while now and my finances were finally becoming stable. It made me so happy to be able to help her out.

"Is two hundred too much?" She grimaced again.

"Done. Two hundred pounds, to Ms Luty." I opened the app and forwarded her the money. "Wow, modern technology, right?" She jumped down from where she was sitting on the bed, walked around and gave me an even bigger hug. "Now you know I charge interest though, right?" I joked and she lightly pinched my arm. We giggled together.

I moved over to the other side of the bed, giving Georgina space to sit next to me. I pulled the tray onto my lap and handed half the sandwich to Georgina. She grinned and took it straight away. We snuggled together as best friends do and watched TV all morning.

The adverts came on and Georgina turned to me. It was like she suddenly remembered something important, which she had been meaning to talk about earlier.

"How are you, by the way?" She asked, in a soft tone, clearly trying not to upset me.

"You mean about Karl?" I replied. She nodded. I moved the now empty tray onto the floor beside her. "I can't deny it, I miss him. After everything we've gone through since secondary school – getting back into each other's lives – it does seem a waste to throw it all away."

"Does he know you feel like that?" She was pushing me to say something, I could tell.

"Well, no. What would it change? He's straight Georgina. He's never going to fall in love with a *girl like me*." I deliberately emphasised the last part of the sentence.

"Look, you don't know that, ok?" I didn't understand why she was pushing this so much. What did it matter to her? "Maybe he's the one? You believe in all that romantic crap, right? Maybe he already does love you?" The curtains blew in the breeze. I felt warm air creep in from outside. Even with the window open and the fan on, it was still very hot.

"I don't know. It's not that easy Georgina. Why do you seem to be so interested anyway? I don't mind, I'm just curious." I turned to face her as I spoke.

"I just want to see you happy. You were happy when you were with him, right? I would hate to see you throw something away because you are scared it might not work. You're too intelligent for your own good. If we all did that, none of us would ever find anyone." She started to raise her voice. She was clearly getting worked up on my behalf.

"Ok, calm down." I looked at her, confused. "Listen, I know breaking up with him seems a waste, but think about it. We can't have sex. I can't have a family with him. His friends and family at the wedding were fucking talking about how much of a monster I was, for god's sake." Georgina looked stunned as I told her what happened. "So look, I don't need that in my life. I want a family and a normal relationship, but I have to be realistic. He deserves a normal girl and I can't be that for him."

"Fiona, don't say that! You are stronger than any other girl I know. You are normal. He would be lucky to have you."

"Well tell him that. I haven't heard anything from him since. It's over. But I'm fine. It has helped me to realise a lot about myself." I smiled at her. I was happy. The happiest I had ever been in my life. "Trust me, me and him, we're over. But it's ok. I will find someone else who understands me and my... situation." I was finished with this conversation. I looked back at the television to silence her. Georgina wanted to keep talking, but my body language was cold.

"Ok. Do you want another tea then?" She said, almost admitting defeat. She grabbed my empty mug and hovered over by my chest of drawers for a moment. I ignored whatever she was doing and watched the TV. Was I being too harsh? I couldn't tell. But it was my problem, not hers. I was finally happy and I didn't want anything to ruin that. Not her, not Karl, not anything.

It had been several moons since the Battle of Sand and Ash as the people of Macha Land had named it. The harsh cold of Winter had returned once more. The Lake had frozen up and formed into the Ice Mountain. The Southern Desert had shrunk down to the Southern Beach. Although the seasons continued to change and the planet had moved on after the Great Battle, many of those living on it had not adjusted so easily to the new world. It would be a long while before all was forgotten.

Across the largest island, the Queen had small willow trees planted where anyone had fallen to the King of Truth's army. It resulted in hundreds of new green patches that stretched down from the centre of the island to the beaches. She often visited them with Prince Hikaru to pay their respects. After the battle was done, Queen Fubuki mourned her beloved mount, but she could not deny the joy she felt when she discovered that Hikaru was still alive. She summoned him as soon as she could after the battle. She was lucky. Most were not. Her realm was reduced to a third of what it once was. Villages were abandoned and the roads remained deserted for days at a time.

"My Queen, it is time." Prince Hikaru held her hand firmly as she walked out from her Palace to greet her people.

"It's good to have you back, my love. We will find the one who attacked you and get your revenge. The King of Truth is no more. There will be nothing to stop us now." Queen Fubuki referred to the large scar that stretched across Hikaru's face, down to his neck. The battle between him and the shadowy doppelganger had reached the point of life and death before the Queen finally destroyed the King of Truth. Any later and Fubuki would have been fated to wear black for every ceremony until her last day. Fortunately, sensing his partner's death, the evil doppelganger had quickly retreated back into the sea. He was still out there somewhere.

"Do not concern yourself with that, my Queen. Your people need you now, more than ever. You must cast the Veil of Warmth before it hails." She wore red silk gloves and a large white coat, with a great, furry hood that covered her head. The coat was pulled in tightly at her waist with a thick red ribbon that cascaded down her front. It danced in the cold winds. She stepped through the snowy floors, staff in hand.

Her people had gathered to see her. Ordinarily, they would watch from the Main Stage, but this time was different. After everything that had happened she wanted it to be more intimate so she invited everyone to come to the Palace. The hill that sloped down for miles to the Main Stage was full of tents and structures erected that day. Hundreds of families had made the pilgrimage to watch the casting of the Veil of Warmth.

Queen Fubuki had aided the Coven of Rosemary to conjure as much food and mulled wine as her people could eat. There were fruits and nuts in bowls. Caskets of ale were stacked atop each other. Wine roasted with cinnamon and other faery spices in barrels were scattered everywhere. Musicians played songs of those who had fallen across the land and collected whatever coins their audience could spare.

After the Great Battle, there was much remorse, reflection and recovery. The Four Guardians had been attacked with the rest of the army and had been forced into the Windy Planes. It took them days to finally leave the everlong storm safely. Upon their return, they each made their apologies to the Queen for not being able to protect her or her people. They were safe. She was glad to hear it. Prince Hikaru was summoned by the Queen when the battle had ended. He fell through the teleportation portal into her arms. For a moment she thought she'd lost him, but her healing magick closed his wounds before she lost him forever.

Many of her people still only wore black. Most of the remaining villagers had fled to the safety of the capital. Centaurs, pixies, halfmen. Every kind of race had joined the Battle of Sand and Ash. Many had perished and those that remained were filled with immense sorrow. Only the early snows turned the air white with hope. Queen Fubuki had prevailed and defeated the King of Truth. Their realm still belonged to them, however much it may have changed.

Prince Hikaru stood back as Queen Fubuki took her place. Her bare feet touched the soft snow, but she felt no cold. Soon, neither would her people. She promised herself that she would never leave the island again. She would stay and protect it. She would have the Four Guardians posted across the rest of the planet if necessary.

"I cast the Veil of Warmth. Atakushi no sekai wo mamotte kudasare!" Her words echoed into the world around her. Her people looked on with anticipation. Their eyes went from her to the skies above them. It was a dark night but the sky was filled with beautiful white stars.

The staff she held glowed with power and emitted a brilliant red light. She span around and pointed the energy to her magnificent, cone-shaped, crystal tower. The light reached out up to the clouds. In the next moment, the light reflected purple and exploded out around the entire island. In an instant the harsh, numbing wind stopped and the people within her magickal island rejoiced. They cheered and shouted with happiness as the celebrations began.

Prince Hikaru walked back over to Queen Fubuki and put his hand gently on her back. They looked out upon their kingdom before them. It was a truly glorious place. It was her world. Her kingdom. No one would take it from her. Queen Fubuki turned suddenly and leant into Hikaru. She kissed him gently on the lips. He felt her body on his as they kissed under the starry sky.

I've tried, but I've failed. I've tried to become her. I've done everything I can, but it's just too hard. The world isn't ready. The looks. The glares. The laughter. I'd rather give up than put up with that for the rest of my life. It's just too much.

My wig is in a knotted pile on my bed. Next to it, my shaver and my makeup. I'm a clown. A fake. A pretender. I wake up every day and cover up his face, just so I can see hers. I just want to be her, not pretend to be her. A huge difference. It is too difficult. I have to give up. I can never be a normal woman. I will never be shorter, or have small feet or be beautiful. The air is heavy and is making breathing twice as hard. There are wine stains everywhere. It's over. I am done with this. I'm weak and I know it. The water is gushing from the taps. I swallow. I drink. I'll become Fubuki instead.

I feel like I've been in this bath water for hours, waiting. The water has lost its heat and I'm cold. My hands are wrinkled and starting to sting. The song is playing on repeat.

"...can't you see... can't you see..."

My slow and tired brain is going over everything. Every person I have ever met. Every emotion I have ever felt, am feeling and am yet to feel. I'm ticking each one of them off, one by one. I will never be able to find love. Never have children of my own. Never be myself. It is not possible. Too late. Sorry. Angel voices from the song echo through the water and penetrate my ears. Her voice eases me into the darkness.

"...in the water... still looking for you..."

I think about her. The woman in my future. The woman I imagine every day. The woman I will never become. I can feel her in my mind's eye. I'm leaving this world and I hope to become her in the next. I have convinced myself that it's possible. The mind is a great, powerful thing and we do not yet know what it is capable of. Perhaps those who believe, end up where they want to be in their afterlife. Who knows. Their own little world. Heaven. Shanti. Nirvana. Wherever I believe I will go, my mind will take me there. I will travel down the river of eternity on my own, just as I came into this cruel world.

The song ends. Then it begins again. Each time, it gets harder and harder to hear it. I will stop hearing it completely soon. Hopefully before I think too hard about what I'm doing and any doubts appear in mind. I am so drunk. I have drunk over three bottles of wine in the past two hours. And the pills. So many pills. Two boxes of painkillers are swimming around my churning stomach. I'll fall asleep any second now, whilst lying in this bath full of water. I can feel myself drifting off. Drifting away. Away forever. I will become her, in the magical world where I am a 'her'.

I'm leaving 'him' behind. I never wanted to be him. I can't carry on being him anymore. It's too painful. It hurts too much. Everyone who has ever loved me, has only loved 'him' and I hate them all for it. I have to say goodbye to him. Goodbye Eric. I feel ready. Ready to become her. Ready to be the person I was always meant to be. In the other world. In my mind. Beyond this realm of existence.

* * *

Another night went by with the sound of sirens filling up the streets of London. A naked male body was rushed in the back of an ambulance to a nearby hospital. After pumping the stomach, the mix of alcohol and pills left the system. They would gain consciousness soon. It would hurt. The doctors had talked to the victim before they passed out completely. After hearing ramblings about wanting to leave this world and going to the next as 'her', they presumed the patient mentally unstable and organised a transfer to the mental ward. For several hours, the pain would continue. When they woke up, the world would be entirely different. A new place. A new person. A new life.

"Do you know your name?" A voice resounded in the room. Where was this room? Where are we? Are we her yet?

Her eyes opened. She had been dead and been brought back to life. The doctors and nurses surrounded her, staring intensely. Her stomach ached, but at least she could feel something. It was time. Across the room she could see a window. Outside the sun was shining through the clouds. Light. Bright and full of hope. It gave her energy. The energy to care. The energy to love. Even to live. The light fell upon her delicate face. It embraced her. Light.

"My name is Beam." She said. Her voice was quivering. A doctor smiled down at her.

"Hello Beam. It's good to have you back. We almost lost you for good there." Another doctor stepped closer to the hospital bed.

"You're back now. Do you understand? You survived." The stranger spoke as if she knew her. She didn't know her. But she had saved her fragile life.

"Not 'survived'… I'm reborn."

The angels kept singing in her head. The song was still playing in her memory.

"*Still looking for you. For you, for you, for you, oh…*"

He was the boy that never truly was and never should have been. She was the girl who fought her way into existence. A soul in a constant battle for peace. They were finally one. Finally as they should be. The body was still the same, but the mind had accepted the truth. She was female. No matter what anyone said, she was female. It didn't matter what her body looked like anymore. This was her second chance to be her true self. This time she wouldn't give up. She would make it this time. With that revelation, her soul grew as light as a feather. The chains of apathy fell away and for the first time in her life she was happy. She was herself. She was alive. She was her.

The sun was shining in the sky and the birds sang to me through my window. In one short year, I had accomplished so much and I was finally allowing myself to feel proud. It was exactly one year since I had been released from hospital after nearly committing suicide. But thanks to a stream of empowering events and what I now like to believe was my destiny I was reborn. That was the beginning of my journey to find myself. My true self.

Classic '80s songs were blaring through the flat as Georgina and I got ready. She was taking me out for a meal to celebrate what she called my "second birthday", as well as to thank me for lending her that money. We kept stopping to dance along to the bass guitars and electro organs. I was in the bathroom, shaving my face as close as I could for the day to come. Georgina was used to that and stood behind me to try and see herself in the mirror.

"How are you doing your hair tonight?" I asked.

"Not sure yet, you?"

"Curling it as usual. Why don't you curl yours too? I think it'll suit you."

"Sure, why not!"

I finished shaving and it stung. I wiped the spots of blood away with a thin layer of moisturiser. After years of shaving so close, I had become very good at it. Nowadays, I didn't get stubble until the next day. The various sessions of electrolysis had started to work. I wiped away the rest of the shaving foam and went back into my room to start my makeup. I dropped my towel to the floor and took a look at my body in my mirror. My boobs had started to grow to a good size. I couldn't go out without a bra on now. Georgina noticed too and kept saying how scared she was that mine would overtake hers soon.

Georgina and I continued to dance to the music as the afternoon passed pleasantly by. It was a Tuesday and Georgina had taken it off especially. She said she wanted to take me to an early dinner, but she was keeping it a surprise. I was excited to be eating at a different location to my restaurant, as I found I ate there all the time on my days off. Paul always gave me a discount. But today was special. It was about celebration.

Georgina finished with the curlers and passed them straight to me. I parted my hair into sections and took my time to curl each bit. My red hair had now grown down to my shoulders and my natural colour had come through by about two inches. It gave an amazing multi-layered look to my hair. When I curled just the red bits it gave me plenty of volume and looked super stylish.

I chose to wear a long red top over my jeggings. It was only a meal in town, it wasn't as if we were going clubbing. She wore a short black skirt that showed off her legs. One day I would be able to wear something that feminine too. Perhaps. We both looked stylish, but also slightly childish despite our age.

We gathered our stuff together and headed out. It seemed a little early to be going out to eat and drink, but it was exciting. It felt thrilling – the journey to the restaurant was longer than I had expected.

"I don't mind or anything, but why did you choose a restaurant so far from ours?" I asked as we changed tube lines for the second time.

"I just really like this place and want you to eat here too. Trust me, it will be worth it. I'm gonna spoil you today, I promise." Something didn't seem right, but I was already having too much fun to care. Maybe she had planned a crazy surprise party with all my family or something. Although that would be weird in the middle of the week.

We finally emerged from the underground at Victoria, when she dragged me onto a train. It all happened so fast that I didn't even glimpse the signs around me. What on earth was she planning?

"Ok, it's the next stop and it's not far from the station at all."

"No problem." I smiled as we got out of our seats, ready to get off. People on the train were staring at us, but for a change I could tell that it wasn't because I was trans. It was because we both looked ready to party. A few guys smiled at us, so Georgina smiled back while I blushed shyly.

Georgina was right, the restaurant was only seconds away from the station. We walked up to the door and I noticed how nice the surrounding roads looked. It was definitely a posh area. It looked familiar. I felt safe and comfortable. She chose well. We walked into what appeared to be an expensive Mediterranean restaurant and Georgina told the hostess her surname. The well-dressed lady nodded and proceeded to walk us to our generously large table. It was in the perfect spot. I sat with my back to the wall, in the furthest corner of the room, so that I could see everyone. We sat down and were handed the menus.

"Did you choose this table specifically?" I had to check.

"Yep!" She looked proud and was glowing with excitement.

"Wow, Georgina, you shouldn't have. I feel like a princess right now!"

"Well good, you deserve it. Look, I know I've said it a million times, but thank you for lending me that money. It really helped me out."

"It's literally no big deal. You don't need to thank me anymore. Actually, from now on, you're not allowed to say thank you for that ever again!" I waved my hands at her like a fairy godmother and she chuckled loudly. The table next to us looked over. Maybe we shouldn't be too loud in this kind of place.

"What can I get you lovely ladies today?" The most attractive waiter I had ever seen was standing by our table. Georgina almost spat her water out when she saw him. I was laughing at her lack of subtlety as she scrambled to look at the drinks menu.

"Erm, can we get two glasses of champagne please? And a bottle of white wine for the table?" That was far too much! She avoided my gaze, cause she knew I would have told her not to worry about champagne just for this. "It's my best friend's birthday, you see. So I want to make sure she has the best time possible."

"I see, well leave that to me then, ladies." He grinned and winked at me. I had to stop myself from blushing. But as hot as he was, I found him a bit over the top. Georgina, however, clearly did not. I watched her eyes follow him back to the bar at the other side of the room.

"All right, put your eyes back in, girl. Bloody hell, you are terrible!" We laughed about it for a while, but before we had time to calm ourselves he was back with the drinks.

"A glass for the birthday girl and for her ever so caring friend." He delicately placed each glass from the tray onto the table. He was balanced and confident holding the glasses from the very bottom. "How young are you, may I ask?" Did he have to ask that?

"She's one year old today, actually." Georgina blurted out before bursting out laughing. I couldn't help but laugh when I saw his confused face.

"What?" The waiter lost all formality and stared at us both blankly.

"She's joking, obviously. I'm twenty something." I smiled. Ok, so I was kind of flirting with my eyes, but barely compared to Georgina. She was literally batting her eyelids at him.

"Well happy twenty-something birthday. I'll make sure you get the birthday treat you deserve for pudding. Are you both ready to order?" He mixed flirting with professionalism. We could use someone like him on our team.

After we ordered, he moved onto the next table. I had ordered the rib-eye steak. Georgina went for the oven cooked mixed fish platter. We decided to share garlic bread as a starter.

It felt so nice to be doing something different. I felt normal. Happy. Not only that, but I felt confident enough to be out, which was great in itself. I didn't feel like I was being stared at, or like I was seen as some transgender freak anymore. It had been a long year, but all in all a very good one.

"So here's to you, Fiona. My best friend. My sister. You're a butterfly, grown from a caterpillar. You've struggled along the way, but you're here now." She paused for just a moment. "And that's what matters. Happy first birthday as the real and fantastic you. I love you. And here's to the next year of wonderful and scandalous times together." Her sudden but heartfelt speech brought a tear to my eye. I quickly wiped it away to stop my eyeliner from running and picked up my champagne glass. The table next to us, who had overheard her speech and I presume had now realised about me, nodded along with the toast.

"Thank you Georgina. Here's to us." I replied with a genuine smile on my face.

We raised our glasses and cheered. It almost felt like everyone was about to get up and give me a round of applause. It was so nice of her. She was a true friend. I couldn't wait to start the next crazy year with her. Who knew what fun adventures we would find ourselves in along the way.

In the next moment I saw him. He was wearing a uniform like the others. What was he doing here? Then it clicked.

"Fuck, Georgina! That's why you brought me here!" I leaned over the table and whispered to her.

"Wait, what?" She turned around to follow my eyeline. "Idiot, he was meant to come out later." She muttered to herself.

"Georgina Luty, tell me right now. What is going on here?" My heart was pounding and I felt sick with nerves. I could see Karl's deep blue eyes all the way from this side of the restaurant. He moved around with drinks in his hand, focusing closely on what he was doing. The waiter from earlier cracked a joke with him and Karl's smile caused my heart to tighten.

"Ok, ok, just relax. Yes, I brought you here on purpose." She admitted. She was about to explain further, but the waiter brought over our garlic bread.

"Here you go ladies, enjoy." He placed it down delicately and then headed back to the kitchen.

"What is this about? Is that why you were asking all those questions the other day?" I started to raise my voice and had to make a conscious effort to calm down with a gulp of champagne.

"Calm yourself. Just listen." She leaned in too. I was still furious though. "Karl added me and messaged me asking about you. He has been really down since you broke up with him. I mean really down. I seriously think he cares about you and wants to be with you Fiona. You just have to let yourself be happy." I went to argue, but she carried on before I could. "He messaged me asking if you missed him at all. Seriously. Boys don't do that. None that I know, anyway. He said if there was a way to get you two together just one more time so he could talk to you, he would do anything." Even though she was trying to sound apologetic, she was smiling with excitement. She enjoyed playing the matchmaker.

"What the hell, this is mental." I felt like the room was spinning. It felt like a romantic comedy gone wrong.

"But to be honest, he wasn't meant to be here yet. Maybe he's early, I don't know. He said he starts work at the bar at seven. It's only half five. Anyway, the idea was that he would come over before his shift started. For dessert he was meant to bring you over a cake with a candle in to surprise you and ask that you take him back. Maybe this way is better though, because it would have been embarrassing if you died of a heart attack like you just did." Georgina joked. I wasn't ready for jokes. I was still angry. But it was a strange anger. At the centre of it, I felt happy. But still angry.

"Georgina I don't know whether I should kiss you or kick you under the table!"

"Do both if you have to. What matters to me is that you don't let this guy slip through your large but feminine fingers." She was trying to make me laugh and despite myself it was slowly working. As I let myself smile, Karl's eyes looked up from the bar and met mine. The room froze but my heartbeat quickened. There he was. Handsome. Kind. Genuine. I wanted so much to be able to trust him. I wanted to let him love me.

"Fiona?" Georgina attempted to get my attention back but I was lost in his eyes. Karl put down the drink that he was mixing. The bartender next to him looked baffled as Karl made his way to us.

"Fiona. Hi." He said when he got to our table. He nodded and smiled thankfully at Georgina, who was failing to hide her grins behind an empty champagne glass.

"Hi Karl. How are you?" I didn't mean to sound as cold as I did. I genuinely did want to know, but my defences were up higher than ever. A part of me just wanted to grab him by the neck and kiss him there and then. But another part of me, the more sensible part, wanted him to leave and avoid this entire situation.

"I'm ok. You?"

"I'm ok, thanks."

"Look, I know this all seems a bit much, getting you here and that. I just wanted to see you. I didn't want to say this by text, but Fiona..." He looked back at the bar and glanced around him. "I want to make another go of things. Sure, we can take things slowly, but I don't want to give up completely. I promise you, I've done a lot of thinking. And I don't care about your situation. I know it's hard for you. I have my worries about the future too, but I... I..." Say it Karl. Say it. "I... Look. Will you at least give me another chance?" We didn't have enough time to talk properly and I could tell he had to get back to the bar.

"To be honest, I still need some time to think about this. Nothing's changed. But I do want to be with you Karl. Of course I do. I care about you. How about we go out some time and talk it out?"

"How about tonight? How about you stay here until I finish and we can grab a drink or two?" His face was full of hope. I couldn't help but smile back.

"Ok. We'll take our time with dinner and I will come to the bar after." I gave in.

"Awesome. Ok. I gotta get to work, but I will see you in a bit. Ok? Then we'll grab a drink somewhere and talk it out. I love you Fiona. Speak to you in a bit. Georgina, thank you so much." His words took me by surprise and I then watched him jog back to the bar. His smile was all I could see.

Georgina was dying to talk to me, but I treasured the moment for as long as I could on my own.

"Did he just say he loves you? Wow. You go girl!" Georgina turned to the white wine.

"He is pretty hot." I admitted to both me and Georgina as she finished pouring.

"Babes, just let it happen. You know, I like to say – anything is possible." She took a long, dramatic sip of wine. We still had our mains to eat and a night of chatting to enjoy. And after that, who knows?

"I guess you're right. Anything could happen."

Printed in Great Britain
by Amazon